Words of Praise for
The Volcano Lady

"A compelling steampunk story with lots of adventure and bits of creative history (Nemo and Nautilus are real!!!) ... Lettie is a great heroine. She is sensible, smart, adventurous, but still aware of her limitations. And then there's Turner, a sigh-worthy character for sure!"
~ *InD'Tale Magazine*

"Highly recommended for fans of science fiction, steampunk, gaslight romance and the tales of Jules Verne."
~*Sharon E. Cathcart, author, <u>Eye of the Beholder</u>*

"Wonderful characters await, each with their own rich backstory, including Captain Nemo! The technology is wonderful, the dialogue totally believable as Victorian and the attitudes as well."
~ *Amazon reviewer*

"(The) Volcano Lady is all about the nature of imagination and how it can exceed reality." ~ *Book Review Mama*

"... a yarn that will draw in fans of alternate-history stories, steampunk fans, or anyone who just loves seeing a determined character go after what she wants ... " ~ *Kindle Reviewer*

"Lettie Gantry does not disappoint us as a true heroine born to set the sensibilities of Victorian womanhood on its ear."
~ *Amazon customer*

Also by T.E. MacArthur

From the Volcano Lady novels:

Volume I – A Fearful Storm Gathering
Volume II – To the Ending of the World
Volume III – The Great Earthquake Machine
Volume IV – The Lidenbrock Manifesto

From the Gaslight Adventures of Tom Turner:

The Yankee Must Die: Huaka'i Po
(the Nightmarchers)
Death and the Barbary Coast
Terror in a Wild Weird West

The Gaslight Adventures of Tom Turner: The Omnibus Edition

Anthologies from Thinking Ink Press:

Twelve Hours Later: 24 Tales of Myth & Mystery
Thirty Days Later: Steaming Forward – 30 Adventures in Time
Some Time Later – Fantastic Voyages Through Alternate Worlds

A GRAY'S ONE SHILLING GAZETTE

The Doomsday Relic

featuring Professor Lettie Gantry

The
VOLCANO LADY

T.E. MacArthur

The Volcano Lady
Gray's One Shilling Gazette #1
The Doomsday Relic
By T.E. MacArthur

©2017 by T.E. MacArthur

All rights reserved.
This book or parts thereof may not be reproduced in any form, stored in a retrieval system, or transmitted in any form by any means without prior written permission of the author, except as provided by the United States of America copyright law.

Cover Artwork / Design: S.N. Jacobson
www.snjacobson.com

Published by: Gray's One Shilling Publishing

ISBN-13: 978-1545320945 (Gray's One Shilling Publishing via Create Space)

ISBN-10: 1545320942

Available in eBook publication and paperback
www.VolcanoLady1.wordpress.com

Line Art attribution
www.Cliparts.co/clip-art-lines.com

The following is a work of fiction. Names, characters, places, and incidents are fictitious or used fictitiously. Any resemblance to real persons, living or dead, to factual events or to businesses is coincidental and unintentional.

Printed in the United States of America

*Dedicated to my cheerleaders and beta readers: to **Laura Ehrlich, Gene Forrer,** and of course my **Papa, Tay McArthur**. With special thanks to my ever-patient editor **Dover** "Put that Semicolon down and back away from the manuscript!" **Whitecliff**.*

*To my writer pals **Sharon E Cathcart** (Eye of the Beholder,) **AJ** and **Belinda Sikes** (the Sometime Later anthology,) **Scott Perkins** (Howard Carter Saves the World,) all the **Authors at Clockwork Alchemy**, and **Karen Krebser** (Poetess extraordinaire.)*

*To **Onyx Calypso the kitten-explorer**, who showed me her secret garden and shares her energies with me. My furry little sister. And to Mac – yes, **Mac the cat**, who was my constant companion for over 14 years and continues to inspire me. My fuzzy Rinpoche. My fighting tiger.*

Brandy Sluss, Roy Nonomura, Deb and **Anthony Kopec; Jay Davis** – I'm not kidding, he truly IS the real Professor Flockmocker, and his lovely wife **Gerri**; **Molly Burke** (the Queen of Confidence); **Adam Lid** and **Karin Mckechnie**; **Juliana Gaul**; and **David Batzloff**. **P.J. Lacy, Dennis Kytasaari,** and **Nancy Schluntz**. The **North American Jules Verne Society** and the **San Francisco Bay Area Steam Federation**.

To the designer of the exceptional cover: **S.N. Jacobson** (www.snjacobson.com.) I am convinced there is nothing he cannot do and each time he proves me right.

To the staff of **A Cuppa' Tea** on College Avenue, who always ask how the book is going and make the best Americanos! To **Edward** and the lovely staff at **Shen Hua** on College Avenue, who make the best modern Asian cuisine and Cosmopolitans.

To everyone who ever said "go for it," "Love your work," or fell in love with Tom Turner as I have.

GRAY'S ONE SHILLING GAZETTE

A Publication Containing the Misadventures of
Professor Lettie Gantry – the Volcano Lady

Issued periodically – By Gray's One Shilling Stories, Novels, and Gazettes. Address, M.R. Gray, Publisher, 36 Dorset Street, Whitechapel, London

---

No. One   London, May 14, 1884   Price 5 Shillings

PUBLISHER'S NOTE

A missive to our readers: Some may be amazed and perplexed at the very size of the novels written in our Volcano Lady series. We agree – they are substantial. So much adventure and knowledge has been packed into each volume that one might not be able to fit it into one's valise – or to lift the said valise containing the tremendous volume. Indeed, dear reader, "volume" appears to be the best word.

Yet, you – our discerning readers – demand quality of detail and excitement. You require exhilarating morsels for your experiential delectation.

Whatever shall we do? Why, we shall bring you instead the Continuing Gaslight Misadventures of Professor Lettie Gantry in proper gazette format, thus allowing your humble publisher to redesign things a tad and present to you this first of many serials to contain the exciting escapades of our plucky heroine.

Oh no! Another cliffhanger? Of course! For what is a life of adventure but a series of cliffhangers and unsolved mysteries awaiting in the near future? We promise to give you resolutions aplenty amidst the thrills and dangers. We promise!

M. R. Gray, owner and publisher

Gray's One Shilling Stories, Novels, and Gazettes
36, Dorset Street,
Whitechapel, London

The Doomsday Relic

A Thrilling Story of Adventures and Dangers

By T. E. MacArthur,
Author of "The Great Earthquake Machine," "The Lidenbrock Manifesto," "The Gaslight Adventures of Tom Turner," etc., etc.

Chapter 1

Yreka Centennial Bank and Loan
California, United States of America

They took it!
No. No!
They took it! They took it!

The older gentleman ran out of the vault holding an empty security box. The look on his face was one of abject horror. He dropped the box, causing already jarred nerves jump once more. People stared at him. He glared back at them, then looked around for the manager – he needed to report what was stolen. It was too important. "Look what they did!"

The bank manager, sporting a sore cheek where he'd been struck and an expression of sympathy for the older gentleman's plight, could only shake his head slowly. "They took everything here – not just yours. Nothing's left."

"You don't understand!" He dropped the box, and pressed his hand against his chest. "This – it was – irreplaceable. It was …" His breath was labored.

Oh, for Heaven's sake, the manager thought. Crazy old man. "Emil, don't get yourself all worked up. Remember what happened the last time."

"It was my life's work."

"And we've contacted the Marshall. He will recover your – whatever it was you kept in there. Don't worry. It will be all right."

"What if the Marshall doesn't find them?"

"You're always digging around down at the mountain. Always coming up with trinkets and stuff. You'll find more."

"Not like this. Not like this! It could mean the end of the world. Do you want to become an automaton? Do you!"

"A what?" Honestly, the old teacher exasperated him at times. "Emil, people lost their savings today. I need to work with the Marshall or we won't get that back. You're getting all worked up over nothing."

Emil Hertford couldn't catch his breath.

The manager was too busy assuring other bank customers that everything would be done to recover their savings to notice.

Hertford knew what was coming. "Frank! For the love of God, I have to tell you …"

"Tell me what, Emil?" He didn't even look at the older gentleman.

"My dig site."

"Mount Shasta, yes, I know."

"No, you don't. You need to know. Someone – needs to – to know …"

Frank the manager assisted an almost hysterical woman out the front door. What else would she be? She'd been held at gun point, robbed of her personal possessions, and then had her entire savings taken away. What would she live on? How would she survive?

"Alright, Emil." Frank locked the door. "Doomsday. End of the World. God Almighty coming down from on high. And your mysterious dig site. Emil?"

The older gentleman, teacher and scientist, lay on the floor.

Frank rushed to see what had happened.

The old man's heart had finally given out.

Damn shame. Emil was crazy but at least he was polite. Sometimes entertaining. He would be missed. And, he never did say where his dig site was; where he got all the trinkets and things Frank rarely actually saw. Emil would tell him all about his latest find, and Frank would pretend to listen.

A knock on the door meant the Marshall and his men had arrived.

That was fast.

Frank stood up and went to the door.

At least twenty men entered – far more than a bank robbery deserved. He looked outside and was astonished to see two small transport airships, bearing Federal seals on their enormous balloons, floating over the Marshall's office.

He suddenly remembered that he'd need to explain to them that Emil was not entirely a victim of the robbery, though perhaps the crazy old man wouldn't have died if they hadn't been robbed. Well, that would raise the bounty on the robbers – they could add murder to the charge, even though none of them shot anyone.

Doomsday? End of the World?

As the multitude of Federal policemen started a remarkable investigation into the robbery, Frank stood by the door – answering questions occasionally tossed at him. Did he hear someone say, "New Confederacy?" Not exactly Doomsday but certainly irritating. Good Lord, what next. A New Confederacy? Some mystery aeroship attacking towns on the East Coast. Rumors of trains that could travel without tracks. What was the world coming to?

None of the Federal policemen seemed to know or care who Emil was, perhaps the crazy old man's trinkets from Mount Shasta weren't what they were looking for. Maybe, Frank thought, they should be.

Chapter 2

Hotel Austen, near the Circus
Bath, Great Britain

Rain poured down as the skies lit up in flashes of lightning, followed too quickly by tremendous thunder. She pressed her back against the chimney and waited – listening. In the distance, down near the river, the slow chugging of a steam engine and the low whistle meant that the last train was departing Bath. Lettie Gantry was trapped on a rooftop, soaked to the bone, waiting to see what would hit her first: a lightning bolt or one of the Prussians trying to capture her.

Few were out in the dreadful weather. It was evening and most good folk were at home by their fireplaces or tucked into bed. Fire. Yes, she could smell all the lit fires, and the chill that clung to her made her envious. Only a determined audience of scientists were willing to brave the storm to listen to a lecture by the infamous Charles Darwin. She was supposed to be there. But she wasn't. She was here – stuck on the roof of her hotel – hiding.

A broken roof tile skittered across the smooth sandstone.

She pressed her back harder against the brick and lifted her pistol in readiness.

A whisper. Male. Two men.

Carefully, feeling the shaking in her body, she leaned around the chimney to look. Pitch dark. Some small lights across the street. Not even shadows.

She crouched down further.

A staccato of flashing light filled the skies overhead.

There they were.

One with a knife.

The other with something. Not a gun.

They were thrust into darkness again as the crackle of thunder roared past them and boomed into the river valley below.

Another flash revealed the men climbing over the divider between the houses, onto the next rooftop. God, they were quick.

The rain was slowing but the storm itself was raging.

She could hear a piano and singing voices underneath the heavy echo of thunder. It was quite warm out, and windows would be open despite the rain.

She would wait. They might go even further along the joined rooftops. It was the fashion of Bath architecture to have connected houses in long rows. Such a design may well have saved her life.

She would wait.

It had only been moments – mere moments – since she'd walked out from the dressing room while securing her blue carnation and found them waiting. At first she thought they were thieves, but then the clean-shaven chins, military crop-cut hair, and thick Germanic accents told her she was dealing with a recently acquired enemy: the Prussians. All that had transpired in Iceland, Admiral Hagan, and how she helped keep Prussia from making the island its own private weapons factory, had not endeared her to the leaders of that country. Why they wanted to kidnap her now – this made no sense.

Yes, when she'd walked into the room, her jacket not yet buttoned, the two men were quite clear; they were kidnappers not assassins. Why her? Surely they didn't like her, but attacking a British citizen in the center of the Empire was a risky way of saying they were put out with her behavior.

Another flash.

Damn it, now she couldn't see them at all.

She couldn't wait longer.

One more flash of light and she could see her escape route.

Lowell of the Foreign Office had told her to stay in London. He probably knew this sort of thing might happen. He should have told her. But Lettie was too determined to show solidarity with Mr. Darwin and the other controversial scientists. She'd worn her blue carnation proudly all day, even when she received ugly stares from disapproving tourists at the Pump Room. She was not going to miss this evening.

No - it wasn't fair to blame Lowell alone. With all her experiences of the past few years, she should have known it for herself.

She had told Lowell that she would not hide from the displeasure of a willfully ignorant general population. Science was too important. Yes, there had been riots. And certainly there would be protests outside the venue where Mr. Darwin would speak. And yes, the rioting in general had become extreme, especially in London. But she assured him she would not hide.

She was hiding now.

Slowly, she stood up. The taffeta of her petticoats were sopping wet and no longer rustled. Keeping her back against the brick, she worked her way back to the window she had crawled out of. She tried not gripping the pistol too tightly. Rain dripped down her hat, hair, and face.

Lightning showed her a clear path to the window.

The hand came up over her mouth.

She smelled them before she could see them.

She could feel the knife.

The man in front took her pistol.

The man holding her whispered in her ear, "Fraulein Doctor, you will with us come. We will leave quietly. I will if I must kill you."

Lettie was pushed and pulled to the partially open window. The first man opened it fully and began to climb through. She was prompted to do the same and after coercing her skirts to cooperate, felt her feet touch down on the floor of her dressing room.

She twisted her wrist out of the man's grip and slammed the window down onto the head then the hands of the man trying to follow them inside. She managed to slam the window down a third time and lock it before she was dragged away.

The Prussian threw her to the ground and tried to reopen the window for his comrade.

Lettie stood up, stepping on her petticoat – tearing it in the rush, and lashed out with the silver powder box from the dressing table. The metal landed brutally on his forehead and sprayed white powder into his eyes and nose. He yelped in pain but kept trying to reopen the locked window for his companion. When she tried to stop him, he seized her by the waist and threw her to the floor again.

Sitting near his feet, Lettie pulled the pin out of her hat and lanced him through the calf. The Prussian howled in pain and fell, grasping at the pin, desperate to get it out of his leg.

The window glass shattered as the other man didn't wait for it to be unlocked.

Unable to see her gun, she scrambled to her feet, gathered her skirts, and ran toward her front door. Outside, she looked around for accomplices and the best route for escape from the hotel.

Down the central, twisting stair case to the second floor.

Her hair was grabbed from behind and her whole body was forced to stop moving. The big hand was over her mouth again, but that didn't stop her from screaming underneath it.

He dragged her to the servant's stairs and shoved her into the stairwell. Closing the door behind them, he essentially cut her off from anyone who would hear them.

"What the devil do you want!" she yelled hoarsely, shocking the man with unexpected language for a modern, civilized woman. "I don't have riches or treasures, nor does my family."

He stared at her for a moment. "You have nothing we want."

"Then why are you doing this?"

"The *Albatross* designs."

"Robur's ship?" she remembered with horror. "The flying ship *Albatross*? I don't know anything about its design. I'm a geologist and mathematician, not an engine …"

The man actually rolled his eyes. "You are worthless, Fraulein. We want the American to tell us. You will write to him. You will tell him to come to you. He will not ignore you, as we know he made you an offer of marriage. He will come and then he tell us. Simple, even for you to do."

They wanted her to use as leverage against Tom Turner. Commander Tom Turner, of the American Navy. Tom Turner of the remarkable blue eyes. And just how did everyone seem to know about Tom's marriage proposal?

"You are out of weapons, Fraulein. Now you will cooperate." He smiled smugly, not once offering to assist her.

Just as she'd been taught, she landed her carefully balled up fist squarely on his nose with a slight upward force. Fast. Brutal. Properly unladylike.

Grasping the balustrade, Lettie swung her weight and foot out to his knee. He barely avoided it. Instead he grasped her around the waist and mouth again.

She bit down hard on his hand.

Her feet reached the wall and she pushed hard.

The Prussian let go but tumbled backward down the stairs.

Lettie slid two steps down, turned, and with her skirt now nearly over her head, stumbled her way back up to the door- and out.

She ran as hard as she could, picking up a bowl of fruit from a corridor table, and slamming the second Prussian, who had managed to pluck her hat pin out of his leg, in the head. He fell back into the wall. Lettie kept running.

Despite best efforts on the part of the Prussians and the continually booming thunder overhead, someone took notice of the commotion in the hallway.

"What's this, then?"

Lettie pushed past the fellow with a flurry of gentile apologies and raced into his hotel room.

His wife looked up in shock.

The window above the street was open, the storm breeze billowing the light curtain. Lettie stuck her head out into the air. A maintenance ladder. It led down to the roof over the first floor, probably over the ball room.

She shoved the window fully open, sat down to climb out when she stopped. The husband and wife were staring.

"Close and lock that door. If two men come in, do nothing to get in their way."

"Is this an assault?" the man asked, drawing himself up boldly. His wife went immediately to the door, closed and locked it.

"These are serious men who are willing to commit murder," Lettie replied. "Please do not do anything to provoke them …" She stopped, astonished, as the man withdrew a blue carnation and a bayonet from his travel trunk . His wife also sported a carnation.

"Major Allister Wilson Thomas Gardner, Royal Engineers, retired. So, anarchists are they? Anti-science? Your path to safety ma'am is quite safe."

Lettie looked down at her jacket. Her carnation of Solidarity with Science was still pinned to her lapel. "Well done sir. But I would ask you to take the safest road."

The Prussians began banging and trying to force the door.

The husband took his wife by the hand and stepped to the corner, out of the way.

Against her urgency to flee, Lettie waited until the door was broken open and at least one of the Prussians could see that she was leaving.

The Prussian with the knife turned on Major Gardner, who responded with military efficiency. Sliced up horribly, the injured Prussian fled back out the door and down the corridor.

The remaining Prussian kept following Lettie.

She pushed her body against the sandstone, hanging onto the ledge by her fingertips and standing on her toes. Her shoes were new and had not been worn down to a smooth sole, which was a blessing. Carefully, she worked her way to the ladder.

Grasping it, she climbed down, slipping a dozen times due to petticoats and rain water. The Prussian was having a harder time of it, but he would still likely make it to the ladder.

She leaped down the last few feet and ran to the edge of the roof. She was right above the street.

The craziest notion entered her head; had the mere receipt of a proposal endowed her with the Turner Luck?

Below, ambling along at an easy pace, was a hay cart. What luck indeed!

The cart was probably heading to the stables near the Royal Crescent.

Blessing the Turner Luck while cursing the man for endangering her life again, Lettie jumped.

She landed bustle first into the scratchy but blissfully soft hay.

The driver turned around to see what had fallen in.

"Can you whip them up?" she asked, grasping the back of the driver's seat. "Go faster if you please!"

The driver looked at the well-dressed but drenched woman, the shadow of a man on the first floor roof, and some wild fellow shouting and waiving a bayonet in the window above. If for no other reason than the tale he'd have to tell at the pub, he faced forward and set his horse to a gallop.

Lettie muttered an exhausted thanks and fell back into the hay.

She hadn't thought of the deceased Robur the Conqueror in a long time and the memory made her shiver. Now the Prussians wanted to use her to force Turner into telling secrets he'd managed to keep for so long? Riots in the streets of London, left over from when the Earthshaker had been sending his manifesto to the newspapers – calling for racial purity and women's subjugation. War on the horizon as various nations lined up on either side of potential battlefields. The world had gone mad.

She needed a vacation. Some months on the side of an active volcano, spewing lava and disgorging pyroclastic flows – in other words, somewhere safer than where she was.

Sitting up, she wondered for a moment if she might still make it to Mr. Darwin's lecture.

Chapter 3

Le Magasin d'éducation et de récréation
The Magazine of Education and Entertainment
(The Publishing House owned by Pierre-Jules Hetzel)
Paris, France

"We were not able to obtain it, Monsieur." The man waited for his superior to speak.

Pierre Jules Hetzel kept writing. Slowly, he put down his pen, looked over at his best author, Verne, who was sitting on the sofa reviewing edits to his latest novel. Verne, for his part, did not respond. The author was used to all this cloak and dagger, Hetzel thought. Verne could have selective hearing when he wanted. Though, as he was frowning and re-reading some comment made on his manuscript, perhaps Verne was merely too engrossed.

The third-floor room had a feel of a well-organized gentleman's club, with dark wainscoting, deep blue paint, white trim, and book cases from floor to ceiling. The ceiling was painted with a variety of stellar constellations and Greco-Roman characters. A smell of cooking pies from across the street floated into the room though a slightly open window. The private office of one of the most successful publishers in France served a variety of purposes, some of which would not be known to the public.

Of course, Verne knew pretty much everything going on – Hetzel allowed him to know.

"Freunde, be very certain the Relic was not simply misplaced by Hertford. Then see if he had any opportunity to …"

Francois Freunde, a man of middling years, with patchy blonde hair and a large moustache, held up a hand to politely interrupt his employer. "We were able to determine that he did not have such opportunity – before he was robbed."

Verne looked up on that note.

"Robbed?" Hetzel asked in frustration. "Can these Americans not control their law breakers?"

Shaking his head, Freunde replied, "No, sir. In fact, out on their frontier, law is not very well established or respected. In particular, we have at least determined that it was stolen by criminals acting on behalf of the so called *Nouvelle Confédération*. I believe Monsieur Verne may have some illumination regarding this rogue entity."

Verne set everything aside and stood up, with some trouble as he'd been sitting far too long. "*Oui*, I do know a bit about them. As you know, Monsieur Turner and I were forced into a confrontation with the New Confederacy last year." Hetzel's expression turned from frustration to interest. "A small band of individuals who want to create days of glory that never really existed. Most were killed but some remain. It would not surprise me to learn that the few survivors had turned to crime to fund their beleaguered cause."

Hetzel sat thoughtfully for a time. "If the Americans wish to have another civil war, that is not our immediate concern. However, if these *Confédérés* are still aligned with the Prussians, this could be of the greatest concern to France." He shook his head and whispered, "never again."

Freunde and Verne waited as Hetzel's mind cleared away memories of bombs falling on Paris from Prussian airships and bullets flying in the villages along the German border.

"Monsieur Verne? May I ask what you are writing now?" Freunde seemed to be genuinely interested.

"Ah, yes. I am writing the definitive adventurous biography of one Jean Robur."

"*Robur-le-Conquérant?*"

"Definitive, official story."

"Was he not Monsieur Turner's employer?"

Verne looked a bit sad for a moment. "It is a very long story, but in short, *Oui*. Turner was among the many soldiers and sailors cast adrift after the great American War. From what I understand, he had little choice and much hope that Robur would be a benefactor to mankind. Alas, this did not come true. Now, Turner is returned to the Navy where he is happy. Robur will become a work of fiction who disappeared, never to be seen again, presumed to be dead."

Freunde nodded in approval. "I will look forward to it."

Hetzel spoke up, mind finally swept clean and focused. "*Merci*. Go back to your team. I will provide you with instructions before you leave. Continue working. We absolutely must have the Relic. Do everything you can."

"There is something else, sir." Freunde squared his shoulders in case Hetzel was not in a receptive mood. "We are hearing reports of strange attacks occurring in America. And it is nothing I believe to do with outlaws and separatists. I don't know if it's related at all to our business."

"Go on," Hetzel waved his hand.

"A small town in the state of North Carolina was briefly terrorized by a ghost vessel – something they claim moved too fast for the human eye to perceive but left a trail of destruction."

"Americans can be easily excited by exotic stories."

Freunde shook his head. "They have sent some of their Federal Policemen to look into it. But found nothing. At first they blamed separatist guerilla fighters, now they say nothing at all."

"You feel they missed something?"

"Something obvious, sir. What was destroyed. A laboratory. The owner, Professor Milton Hennessey, was experimenting with hydraulic capacities – he hoped to apply his discoveries to mining operations. Now he's dead and his work has been obliterated. Another such attack, by a craft moving unbelievably fast, was reported by a Sheriff in the state of Ohio. A brilliant mathematician with hopes of creating better fuels for steam engines. Dead. His laboratory gone."

For a long time, Hetzel rolled several ideas around in his mind. "For now, I do not think they are related incidents. But all the same, you will monitor the situation."

"Yes, sir."

Verne mentioned casually to Freunde, "… And avoid certain Americans. They will not be as sympathetic to France, and will be quite annoyingly honorable while opposing you."

Hetzel nodded in agreement. "That is an entanglement I wish you to avoid if possible."

"We are still speaking of Monsieur Thomas Turner?" Freunde asked.

Verne smiled.

Hetzel frowned and reluctantly nodded.

Chapter 4

The American West

It was simple: rob the bank – give the money to the Cause – keep a small amount for himself. So, so simple. They made everyone sit on the floor, near the teller's station. He and his cousin, once removed, stood watch while their third man went with the bank manager into the vault. This was the day that he, Homer Shadrich, would earn a place of honor in the New Confederacy.

The customers had been separated into two groups. The one behind and to the right of him was mostly made of up older folk, and one especially shabby man – possibly a prospector. Maybe he had some gold on him, but there might not be enough time to search him. The one in front of him had simply dressed men and women. All of them appeared scared.

It was fun, and especially satisfying when he noticed a dark-skinned woman holding her swaddled baby, trembling amongst the customers. Homer looked out over the top of the handkerchief that covered most of his face. What he saw made him seethe. How dare she?

How was it that a Negro girl could afford to wear a white cotton dress, pretty and fancy, and to walk into any public building where his wife couldn't? How was it that some darkie had money when he didn't? She was nothing more than an ape, a mistake of God, marked right down to her skin as something less than human.

Well, if he had anything to say about it, she would never feel free to walk anywhere, not in his country. Never in the New Confederacy. Maybe she didn't deserve to live. No loss if she and that nappy brat died.

Homer raised his rifle and pointed it at the mother and bundled child. "Get up!"

"Leave her alone," one man said before being silenced by the butt end of Homer's rifle.

"I said, get up, you lazy ape. And keep that thing quiet or I'll blow its brains out."

Slowly, the woman stood up. She was thinner than a mother should have been so soon after giving birth but then maybe the baby was smaller than it should be. Her face was impassive. Didn't she have sense to know she was about to take a righteous beating? Maybe die? She was kind of pretty, with almond shaped eyes, but her lips were too full and her skin imperfect.

It was the hat. Yes, it was the hat that made him angry. His wife had wanted a pretty little hat just like that, to perch on the top of her dark blond hair. Instead, he bought potatoes and beans, because that was all he could muster. Until now …

The hat was green with a small set of flowers on the crown band and a pair of little feathers. "Take it off. Take off the hat and throw it down here."

Homer's immediate companion turned to him and smacked him in the arm. "Leave off the darkie. We don't need hats, we here for money."

"She shouldn' be dressin' above her betters. It ain't right."

"Calm down."

Homer turned back to the mother and gestured with his gun for her to take off the hat. Quietly, without changing her expression, holding the baby with one arm, she reached up, pulled a hat pin free, and slipped the hat off her head. She held it out so that he could see it.

He felt himself shaking with satisfaction. "Now drop it!"

But she didn't. She just stood there. The hat teetered up and down in her hand, but she wouldn't drop it. "Are you too stupid to follow commands? I said drop it!" He couldn't take his eyes off the moving hat. It was almost mesmerizing. "Drop it, now!"

As if responding to his demand, a metal ball dropped heavily onto the floor, then rolled to his feet.

He stared down at it as it was a very odd thing. Not at all smooth, but lined as if sliced like an apple around the core. Bronze. Maybe someone dropped it and he could keep it along with everything else he'd been collecting all month. He bent over slightly, to pick it up.

The ball sprung open and surrounded him in a cloud of something foul smelling. His eyes teared up. His companion started coughing. Though it dissipated in seconds, he knew the damage was done. He couldn't get his balance, everything was blurry …

"Why don't you 'drop it?'"

The question came into Homer's left ear on a hot breath, followed by the distinct feeling of a gun barrel prodding him in the neck, just behind his earlobe.

His companion turned to try and see what was happening to him. Before either man could so anything, the mother dropped the pretty little hat, took three long strides, and pulled out of the baby swaddling a Smith & Wesson .44 revolver. She stuck it into his companion's temple. "I've got this one, Commander," she whispered with a slight Creole accent.

"Thank you, Agent. My apologies for being tardy." The man behind Homer reached around to the rifle and yanked it out of his hand. Then he did the most audacious thing; he gave it to the woman. To the Negro woman.

Clearly, she knew how to handle it as well as the revolver.

The third man in Homer's robbing party emerged from the vault with arms filled with bags of money. "What's goin' on out here?" Too many bags. His gun was holstered and there wasn't a chance in hell he'd be able to reach it in time.

They'd been had.

That bank was an easy target they'd been told. Quick money. Homer looked down at the green hat on the floor and realized he wouldn't be home to his wife for a very long time.

Five uniformed men rushed into the bank and began wrestling Homer, his companion, and money-bags man to the ground. He looked up to see the Negro woman standing over him, with the same impassive expression, handing over his rifle to the authorities – as evidence, she said. Did she feel nothing? She'd just ruined his life.

"Again, my apologies for being slow," the Commander said, stepping back from the chaos of the arrest. Homer could see him now: it was the shabby prospector. A Commander?

Finally, the woman's impassive face broke away for a smile. "Not to worry. I've dealt with these sorts all my life. I wasn't in danger yet. These boys …"

How dare she call him a boy, Homer opened his mouth to say.

"These boys are cowards on the inside." She sighed, then picked up and put the green hat back on, clearly satisfied with it.

"Bet you didn't expect that purchase to be so handy?"

"Oh, Commander, I think everything is a potential asset in a fight, even if it's pretty."

The Commander laughed and offered the woman a friendly handshake. Homer wasn't sure what was going on now, but surely the world had come to an end if a white man was so quickly offering his hand in congratulations like that.

"My thanks again for holding them the extra time while we got into position."

"My pleasure and my job. That's what I was in here for."

Homer was forced onto his feet and finally got a good, long look at the man who had snuck up behind him. The shabby coat and damaged hat were a disguise. Now he could see a patch of glue where the shaggy beard was glued into place. All a costume. A pair of intense blue eyes glared at him, declared him a piece of garbage, and then dismissed him. Homer began shouting, "God bless the New Confederacy!"

"It'll take more than God," the woman said.

The two watched silently as Homer and his failed heist companions were dragged out of the bank. As other customers were assisted to their feet, told their savings had not been stolen, assured that this would never happen again, and sent home, the two watched and waited.

Once the bank was cleared of all civilians except the manager and a teller, who were engaged in providing details to one of the uniformed men, the Agent and the Commander looked at one another, deciding whether to laugh or not. Since they were quite safe to speak without risking greater exposure, they both visibly relaxed.

"Commander – that beard is horrible and you didn't glue it on very well. Just because they're stupid doesn't mean they're entirely stupid. One of them might have noticed if you had to stall for more time."

The Commander began pulling off the beard, with strings of glue stretching out and finally surrendering to the pull. "Beggars can't be choosers." Underneath was a bit of stubble, but an otherwise pleasant face. With the false beard out of the way, however, the Agent likely saw that infamous scar around his neck. She had told him earlier that she knew the stories – she knew how and where he got it. It was a badge of honor in her eyes. Turner had been very flattered if instantly uncomfortable.

"Commander, I'm nonetheless grateful you helped us follow through with this little operation."

"Agent Jefferson," he said, likely never to know her real name, for safety's sake, "I'm pleased to be of help." There was something very satisfying in knowing that her fellow agents used the names of presidents for cover. He thought it was quite comfortably ironic. "We knew that Homer Tannery was one of the men involved in the New Orleans Naval Yard robbery – he's not as bright as he thinks he is. He pretty much led us here and to one of the meeting spots for the New *Seceshs*. Apparently, you and yours came to the same conclusion and were already here. One stone and we've killed that proverbial pair of birds," he said.

"Well, when I'm old and telling stories of my wild young days, I'll surprise everyone when I tell them about the day the Navy came and saved this little land-locked town."

"Assisted — we only assisted an existing operation." Commander Tom Turner smiled, lopsided, and added, "And I think all your stories will be considerably more interesting than this one little episode."

Agent Jefferson looked over Turner's shoulder, toward the door and he followed her visual cue to see a Lieutenant, in informal uniform, emerge from the mixed crowd of policemen and navy personnel, and walk directly into the bank. He was quickly followed by a remarkable man, dressed in a leather apron, rolled up sleeves, heavy canvas leggings, and all sorts of odd equipment sticking out of his bowler hat.

"Commander," the Lieutenant said, ignoring the oddly dressed man who pushed past him.

"Lieutenant." Turner realized he needed to show some decorum, despite nearly everyone in shouting distance belonging to some sort of mutual security force. "Agent Jefferson, I don't believe you had an opportunity to meet my right-hand man. Lieutenant, this is Agent Jefferson."

Albert Forrer tugged on his hat, a field salute, and nodded politely to the Agent. Of course, Forrer wasn't taken off guard by the presence of a black government agent. And a woman too. Forrer and Turner were always playing some sort of one-upmanship in the arena of "who has seen it all" now. Turner was never sure if Forrer took the same delight in seeing a post-Civil War society becoming better blended, but then, Forrer was much younger and perhaps his generation was blissfully un-acknowledging of the past. Either way, it was pleasing for Turner to note Forrer's lack of surprise.

It was his dream, and he knew it wasn't very likely to happen, that everything that caused the Civil War would simply melt away into oblivion. Well, his position with the *Old Men* – a handful of Union generals and other broad-minded individuals who used their vast experience to protect the United States from all those innumerable enemies foreign and domestic – had him living in a socially protected arena. Not that his safe bubble wasn't burst frequently, but he could always count on retreating into it whenever he wanted to. The rest of the world – well – that was another situation, one that allowed a New Confederacy to rear its ugly head.

Agent Jefferson began watching the oddly dressed man as he circled the remains of the bronze ball on the floor. "Is *he* also one of yours, sir?" she asked.

"Ah, yes, he is. Haven't given him an operational name yet."

The oddly dressed man looked up, tipped his hat to the agent, and went back to scrutinizing the bronze ball. "You used it. I told you not to use it. There aren't sufficient chemicals …"

"It worked just fine. We were a little pressed for time," Turner said. He was going to hear about this all the way home. He couldn't help but chuckle as the odd man put on heavy gloves and carefully picked up the opened chemical ball as daintily as one might a piece of sheer bone china.

"I'll want a report," the man demanded.

"I know," Turner said, with little enthusiasm.

"But first, sir, a message from Home." Forrer handed Turner a small envelope, as if it might be a source of relief.

Agent Jefferson likely knew she wasn't privy to their secret dealings any more than they were to hers. It was how the game was played. That was what her expression and the two steps back suggested. "New orders, Commander?"

"Very likely."

"Well then," she said extending her hand in a way her father never dreamed of. "May I wish you success and again, our thanks for your assistance?"

Forrer glanced over his shoulder at the street. "We may need to take the back exit. I must wonder how many folks are glad we came. Ah – beyond yourself, ma'am."

The woman nodded. "Most, I would say. Oh, they don't always know what to do or say to people like me, but I think most folks aren't interested in going back to the old days." She looked at the milling crowd and frowned a bit. "Still, you may have a point Lieutenant. I'm certain my participation will be well known by the end of the day, but then, I don't live here and few would be able to pick me out of a crowd in the future. I won't be able to walk out the front door, and you, Commander Turner, should keep your identity safe and secret."

"Agreed. Thank you again."

"And to you, sir." She smiled to Forrer as well. "Lieutenant."

The odd man with the bomb fragment called back a pleasant if disconnected "Madam, good day."

Out the back door of the bank, Turner kept pulling pieces of theatrical glue off his chin.

Forrer kept up with him, looking back at the bank frequently. "So that's the Secret Service?"

"Part of it. Some agents are public and some, like Agent Jefferson, are kept relatively hidden so that they can do their job covertly."

"Hence the name Secret Service. I'm sort of surprised we don't work together more often."

"We may, Forrer. This was just one more robbery intended to fund the New Confederacy. It may get plenty worse before it gets better." And just for the fun of it, he called after the odd man and his bomb fragment still dangling from the enormous gloves, "Don't drop it, Flockmocker."

If Flockmocker was capable of such base vulgarity, he might have made a gesture of reproof to Turner, but instead, he kept walking quickly ahead of them.

Stuffing his hands in his pockets, looking for a handkerchief for the sneeze he was obviously fighting as it lingered behind his sinuses, Forrer asked, regarding the envelope, "Your orders or *ours*?"

There was something he liked about Forrer, and it was something he'd not appreciate in any other officer, sailor, or soldier; they'd been through too much together to be anything but frank. Of course, when they'd met, Turner had been an injured civilian and Forrer the superior. Now, tables had turned, and it was Forrer who answered to him. It was certainly not something that happened commonly in the military.

Turner stopped to open the envelope and began to read the message inside. "Mine – I think …" He read the note over and over.

"What is it?"

"I'm needed to look into some strange attacks happening up and down the East Coast. This has been going on for quite a while. A friend of mine," he immediately remembered the smiling, white bearded face of Jules Verne, "was going to see for himself. He didn't find much and headed back to France. It would seem things have now changed from curious to dangerous." He looked up at Forrer, who appeared to be both concerned and excited. "Have a look at this – someone took his cue from the Earthshaker and has started writing letters to the newspapers. With all the riots and madness going on over in England, let's just say the Old Men are concerned."

Turner withdrew a cut newspaper article from the envelope, read it, and handed it to Forrer – with a tremendous desire to roll his eyes or throw his hands in the air out of frustration.

Carefully holding it, Forrer stopped briefly while reading it.

Great Eyrie, Blueridge Mtns,

To Mr. Strock
Federal Police
34 Long St., Washington, D. C.

Sir,

You were charged with the mission of penetrating the Great Eyrie.

You came on April the twenty-eighth, accompanied by the Mayor of Morganton and two guides.

You mounted to the foot of the wall, and you encircled it, finding it too high and steep to climb.

You sought a breech and you found none.

Know this: none enter the Great Eyrie; or if one enters, he never returns. I give this warning to all, not just to you.

Do not try again, for the second attempt will not result as did the first, but will have grave consequences for you.
Heed this warning, or evil consequences will come to you.

Commander, Master of the World

"The Master of the what?"

Turner shook his head.

"Well, let me know if I can help, sir. I'd be proud to take another assignment from the Old Men. I have time – I've not received new orders to take me away from this work."

"Then pack up. We're heading East. This could be a long assignment"

Forrer looked at him. "But …"

"I'll have new orders issued."

Forrer started walking.

"Unless something has changed, I still get to pick my staff, it's a necessity of the job. Unless you don't want …"

"Yes, sir. Train station. Five minutes. I intend to beat you there, sir."

"… unless you don't want to join me."

Forrer's expression reiterated his answer.

"Glad to hear it."

The Lieutenant nodded sharply with a wide grin. It was Turner's guess, but he was willing to bet that Forrer was already packed up, since he never seemed to unpack, no matter how long he expected to be in a location for an assignment. Or maybe, the Lieutenant was simply that excited about what he might do next and didn't want to waste time.

"Would you tell me one thing, sir?"

Turner stopped and waited.

"And I ask this, sir, because you accidentally made it my business."

"And that is?"

"It is a tad personal. We have an excellent working routine, but you are still my Commander and I am …"

"And, Lieutenant?"

"Did she ever send you a reply? Or is that why you're out here taking every dangerous assignment the *Old Men* or the War Office can send you on? Remember," Forrer added when Turner began to protest the Lieutenant's intrusive question, "I helped you write and send the Tipsy letter to her."

"You're banking on our friendship …"

"I'm checking to see where your thinking is. I'll follow you anywhere, friendship or no. I only want to know what I'm signing up for – I prefer knowing the facts. I'm better at serving with the facts."

Turner's annoyance dissolved quickly, as if it hadn't existed in the first place. "I'm not trying to work myself to death, so don't worry. No suicide missions – at least, not on purpose."

Forrer waited.

"No. She didn't. And, I'm quite fine with that."

Forrer kept waiting.

"No, truly I am. I'm a realist."

Forrer didn't move. That was Forrer: he said more in silence sometimes. And, he was right; Turner had leapt into his new duties with a tad too much gusto. Personally, he'd chalked it up as being enthusiastic about his new life. It wouldn't be the first time he'd been wrong.

"Really. Truly. I am absolutely fine with it."

Liar, Turner thought to himself.

Chapter 5

New Mexico Territory

The young man, really still a boy except for his remarkable, if not surprising, gift for mathematics, stayed put where he'd been dropped. Lantern lights flashed on the ground as men raced by him, running toward the burning building. He was still in shock. It had all happened so fast.

One minute, he was saying good night to family friends and telling his father he needed to fetch his books from Mr. Nicols's laboratory, where he'd spent so many happy afternoons learning and avoiding chores. He loved the place and it was there that numbers had taken on new meaning. The inventor made calculations and formulas fun. The inventor recognized talent in the boy which no one else noticed.

The next minute, he was being dragged toward a vehicle the likes of which he'd never seen before. Another minute more and he was sprawled under the boardwalk in front of the Marshall's office, right where his father had thrown him – for his own safety. The inventor and his inventions were lost in a ball of flame. The vehicle and would-be kidnappers had sped away at tremendous speed. Half the town was trying to put out the laboratory fire; the other half had gone with his father to chase down the vehicle.

Why did they want him? He was just a rancher's son. And yes, the kind inventor – one Mr. Nichols – had told him he was a genius in the making. But certainly, he wasn't close to tapping that potential. The math and the engines – they were fun; that was all. Frankly, all the young man wanted was to write, like Mark Twain, or to become a surveyor, or maybe just a good cattle rancher like his father. But the world had been changing with a different future presented to him.

Slowly, he crawled out from under the boardwalk. The danger was gone and he knew it.

He couldn't have stood more than five feet and a couple of hands tall. Thin by nature. Medium brown hair and big, boyish eyes. He was not a miniature of his father but rather his mother. He was still so young – his voice hadn't changed and there wasn't yet any stubble on his chin. Until that moment, he was rather content with the state of things.

The Marshall, whose first duty was to get the fire under control, since they had no actual fire brigade and the rest of the sleepy town was under threat of obliteration, conducted an orchestra of volunteers passing buckets of water to the site. Even the usual drunkards, cowhands, and gamblers set aside their needs to help.

The young man stood, staring at the building, seeing through the flames the memory of a building that had once been a horse barn. Mr. Nichols, with his bright eyes, yellow hair, and frequent smile, telling him about the workings of the steam engine, medical uses for independently operating machines such as the one a Professor Pierce had invented, and so many other miracles. The bottles of hydraulic fluids to be verified for efficiency. Drawings and models of locomotives. Parts of a wooden manikin that the inventor had used to test some of his own medical innovations. A candy store full of the things boys dream about.

Everything gone.

A tear began falling down the young man's cheek. He wiped it away, remembering someone telling his father that he was much too sensitive a boy. He wanted to be strong like his father.

What would his father do in his place? He would have fought the kidnappers. The young man decided right then and there he needed more rifle practice and to ask his father to teach him to fight. After tonight, his father wouldn't say no.

What would Mr. Nichols do in his place? Get the details. Record everything and have the most accurate description as evidence.

He ran into the Marshall's office, tears starting to flow beyond his control. Taking up a pencil, he began to draw the vehicle, on the back of a wanted poster. The greatest salute to the murdered – yes, murdered – inventor was to put his lessons into practice.

The vehicle was bird shaped. Wood, but not quite. Wings. He remembered the glow of lights that penetrated the covering on the wings. It had been so fast – too fast – maybe he wasn't remembering straight!

He closed his eyes tightly, squeezing the memory out of his brain.

Yes, he saw light through the wings, so they must be made of something like canvas between the "bones" of the structure. Wheels. Not feet. Wheels. He hadn't seen the tail but he was sure there had been one. And the Gatling Gun, near the nose. The sound – he waved his pencil around as if scaring off any noises that might distract him. The sound was of an engine, like the train he'd ridden to Denver last year. A solid hiss. Lights inside the body, where they had tried to drag him.

He kept sketching wildly. It wasn't perfect, but it was close.

How many men? Two had grabbed him by the arms, one was shouting, one was holding an object that burst out a stream of flame. Flaming fuel, because fire did not travel on the air, it needed a fuel. The object was a mechanism that held the fuel in a barrel strapped to the man's back, and a hose of sorts, to spray the destruction.

Now the tears were flowing for Mr. Nichols, but the young man's anger was pushing past it all.

"Boy, what are you doing?" The Marshall walked in, covered in soot and sweat. "You were told to stay put!"

"I saw it, sir. I saw what killed Mr. Nichols." He didn't entirely look up.

"We all saw the fire, boy. It's out now." The Marshall shook his head at the boy sketching. "No time for fantasies …"

The young man held up his drawing with one hand and wiped his face clear of tears with the other. "This is not a fantasy. This is what killed Mr. Nichols. Not the fire – this!"

For a long time, the Marshall looked at the drawing. There were elements he recognized too, though not nearly with such detail, and he said so. For another long moment, he seemed to hesitate with something he wanted to tell the boy. "Look here. Tell me true – you look in any of my papers there?" He pointed to a stack. "It's important. Did you?"

"No, sir!" What did his papers have to do with anything?

"Then I want you to look at this." The Marshall pulled the stack of wanted posters, letters, and notices into the middle of his desk. He quickly flipped through it, the breeze created blowing his one remaining strand of dark hair on otherwise gray head around his face. He pulled out one sheet. It was printed on better paper than anything else in his office. The young man noted the impressed letterhead as he could see the marks pressed through to the back.

The Marshall laid the paper next to the boy's drawing.

The two drawings, side by side, nearly matched.

The boy sat back in the Marshall's chair, staring at the notice from the Federal Police, and warning of attacks from a secretive vehicle. Any sightings were to be reported immediately to Agent J. Strock, Washington DC.

Chapter 6

Denver & Rio Grande Station
Denver, Colorado, United States of America

The train was impressive, but Turner found himself distracted by the shinier objects falling out of the sack than yet another advanced-technology locomotive. It was his indifference to the impressive steam train that was likely agitating Flockmocker. He'd have to explain it to the Professor – later – out of kindness. He'd seen it all before.

Perhaps not this train, with its all-in-one design. Very much to be expected from Flockmocker. All the comforts of home were to be found, attached at various places around the passenger car. Unsurprisingly, the car included remarkably cozy chairs and couches, all upholstered in a clashing cacophony of patterns and colors, as if each had been taken from a different, excessively decorated home. For all Turner knew, the Professor had simply picked them up by the side of the tracks as he and the train's crew tested the engine. Yet, for all the typical, modern, clashing items inside – making the whole thing feel like an upward hopeful, middle class home desperate to show all that their wealth could acquire – the exterior of the all-in-one was sleek. Someone else had a hand in that, Turner thought, noting a few innovations he'd have to remember when complimenting Flockmocker later.

For the moment, he focused on the contents of the sack. Agent Jefferson had kindly handed over the possessions of the robbers – after the Secret Service had its own pick through, of course. There were the expected sets of silver plate ware, no doubt ready to catch a fair price on the market. A pair of now shattered vases, possibly Ming, which caused Turner's stomach to tighten a bit in pity. And this one, strange thing. It came in a box of its own, wrapped carefully in several layers of dirty cotton and rags. It smelled strange – possibly why the Secret Service left it for him.

The engineer, who went by two initials which he absolutely refused to explain, crinkled his nose. "AG" leaned over Turner's shoulder. "Looks like you got the best of the pickings." He stood up. A strongly built man, in his late fifties or early sixties with no sign of retiring from the strange world of technology and secrets. What had been dark, curly hair was now white, but it suited him and made his deep-set, brown eyes even more intense – when he wanted them to look intense. Turner always suspected he'd been in the Secret Service at its inception, but had since moved on. "We'll be leaving in half an hour. Be sure to secure everything – we're still working out kinks in the initial gearing – we'll start off a little rough."

Forrer sat down next to Turner and began cataloging the contents, oblivious to Turner's new obsession. "Why these things? Surely they couldn't be sold for enough money to fund anything substantial."

Turner moved the object back and forth in his hands. Absently, he replied simply, "They can be used to get money for ammunition or rooms while they are preparing for bigger targets …"

"… banks."

"Uh-huh."

"Say, Commander, what is that thing you're staring at?" Forrer pointed and waved his hand under his nose, as though that might help with the odor.

"I'm not sure." He began removing the bandages wrapped around the package. The first ones were cotton and carried most of the stench. "Someone doesn't want others looking too closely."

"How could they see," Forrer complained. "The smell alone is making my eyes water. What on earth is in there?"

The contents landed with a thud. Iron. Lovely. A seated figure, feminine, wearing a crown topped with a large obelisk. The face was of a lioness. A single chariot wheel was attached to the figure's right. There was no sign that a wheel had ever been on the left, which struck Turner as being rather unbalanced for a statue.

Forrer sat down. "What are those tubes sticking out of it?"

Turner said nothing. His eyes grew wide and he was certain that he heart was racing. He knew what it looked like. He knew what it was the artist had created.

"Looks Egyptian," Forrer said with a shrug, "but that's highly unlikely. Who out here would have such a thing? Is it a fake, you think?"

Turner wouldn't let go of it, and Forrer, after initially trying to remove it from his hands, knew better and waited.

"Sir?" He waited. He had learned to be patient and to allow Turner to react, if only to decipher what that look on Turner's face meant.

It might have been a full two minutes before Turner could organize his comments into something coherent – something that didn't sound like it came from a delusional paranoiac. "Forrer? Do you remember seeing any of Hetzel's men – when we were in Hawaii?"

"Not at all. Well, a few blurry memories but nothing definitive. Why? Does this thing look like one of Hetzel's…?" He didn't need to finish the sentence – he'd guessed already. "They look like that?"

Turner could imagine the ideas running through the Lieutenant's head – he'd had the same visions. The tubes of hydraulic fluid to make the mechanical body replacements work. The pain – for surely there was no way to alleviate the pain of having metal parts grinding against bones, exposed skin, nerves …

Forrer tried to shake off the idea. "The object is beautiful. It looks very typical for Egyptian statuary. I've seen others in the museums, but none of them had these tubes." He screwed up his face. "The mechanical men look like that?"

"Some. It depends on how they looked before the mechanical enhancements and what needed to be replaced." His thoughts went to that moment not all that long ago, in the Javanese jungle, at the crash site of the *Albatross*. To his incomplete memory of Robur. Captain Jean Robur, inventor, genius, creator of the flying clipper ship *Albatross* and the smaller – potentially deadlier – *Indomitable*. Madman, commander, rescuer, friend – corpse. Betrayals had led to the destruction of the great flying ship, one of which Turner was convinced he had perpetrated on Robur – to protect Lettie Gantry. It was all a sordid and sad affair, in which no one achieved anything like a happy ending. He lost his commander and friend; Lettie respectably chose her volcanoes over him; Robur lost his life – or did he? It was all so uncertain and unclear.

Had Hetzel actually been there – in the East Indies – and taken Robur's body to have it enhanced? No, Turner told himself. No, it had been a fevered dream.

"Why would anyone make a statue, in an Egyptian style, with those things sticking out of it?" Forrer broke into Turner's thoughts.

He'd been so caught up in his memories that he hadn't noticed Flockmocker standing next to him and staring at the object. Flockmocker could be called any number of things, all of them accurate, but the one that fit him best was *eccentric genius*. He was always cleaning something with a rag and stuffing tools into the pockets he'd sewn into a leather apron – his uniform of choice. "Lieutenant," he addressed Forrer in that pitched vocal tone of his, "I've seen some of these fellows of Hetzel's up close. I'd say we're looking at an object that surmises improvements to enhancement."

Both men stared at him.

In exasperation, he shoved some odd tool into an upper pocket and pointed. "Hetzel was an interesting employer, all two years I agreed to work *with* him, not *for* him," he emphasized. "Never got to see the lab where all the ugly work happened, that was up in his airship, but I saw the results. Most of them were so grateful to still be alive they'd do anything he ordered them to. 'Course, some of them also lost their minds in the process. Nasty business. Wrong use of the technology if you ask me. It's the sort of thing that should have helped veterans replace limbs lost in battle – that sort of thing."

"So this madman," Forrer sat up, "has built an army of insane, mechanical soldiers?"

Strangely, Flockmocker shook his head. "Not quite like that, son. It's more complex. Hetzel is a patriot. He's also one of the first enhanced men – saved his life. But he's anything but mad. He's focused. He's determined. And somewhere in his plan he genuinely wants to protect his nation and its people. I wouldn't have spent ten minutes with him otherwise."

Turner nodded. "Fair point."

"Is it an army he built? Not at first – I think that evolved along the way. But you boys should take a real look at this thing." He snatched it up from Turner's hands. "If those are bio-mechanics, they're subtle – beautiful. They look like the sort of developments I wish had been part of Hetzel's technology – repairs and revitalization of the injured or deformed." He turned the object over in his hands. "With your permission, Commander, by which I mean, I'm going to do this – please don't stop me – I'm going to take a scraping of the metal. I want to see what this is really made of."

Turner held up his hands. "I won't argue, but in case it is an antique, try not to destroy it."

Flockmocker gave him an evil glare, and pulled out a sharp tool. On a clean handkerchief, he scraped some of the bottom of the relic. Not much came off, and he tried two more tools before an adequate sample could be achieved. Returning the object to Turner, he folded the sample up into a tight square and pocketed it.

"It begs a few questions: who made this, why did they make it, why Egyptian, and what does it represent?" Turner began lightly re-wrapping the item. "Knowing what it's made of can help, but I believe we need more expertise. An antiquities expert perhaps – to tell us that this isn't all that old but what it might have been copied from?"

"Who says it isn't an antique?" Flockmocker blurted out.

"You're joking, right?" Forrer asked.

"Why not. You think all them ancient folk were stupid? You ever wonder what all us over-thinkers would achieve if asked to build something like the pyramids? A mess, that's what. We'd never get it done, or we'd do it the hard way just to prove we could do it the hard way."

"That's ridiculous. It's an example of bio-mechanics. Building a building, no matter how tremendous in size, is not the same thing as putting a man back together with metal parts and making that work."

Turner stopped wrapping and stared at Forrer. "It's a map."

"Geographical?"

"Biomechanical. This is a diagram of how to do it. I don't think the age of it matters nearly as much as what it represents. Indulge me for a moment. What if someone found a way to make bio-mechanical enhancement cleaner or easier? You don't remember those that showed up in Hawaii …"

"Well, now that you mention it, wasn't that pirate one of them? His jaw, and now I'm remembering some of the tubes." He looked over at Flockmocker. "I was a little distracted at the time. Someone stabbed me. Anyway, what I remember wasn't elegant at all. It was messy. Obvious."

"Definitely not elegant like this. What if this is the next step? Forget why it looks like an ancient statue – genius comes in very unexplainable forms."

"Thank you," Flockmocker said, polishing another tool for no good reason.

"What if this is the next step – an evolution, as Mr. Darwin might suggest – of bio …"

A deep thump drew their attention to the passenger door.

Shadows moved across the windows as the train sat still. That wasn't good. Turner and Forrer looked up then to one another. Without saying a word, they waited, listening. Whoever was outside had no interest in staying quiet.

AG entered the room, held up a hand to indicate he wasn't going to make any noises. Yes, the man had experience. From inside of the bib of his overalls, he removed a small pistol. Good man, Turner thought, slowly moving toward the back of the car, his eyes never leaving the shadows on the window.

Forrer lifted a Colt out of his bag and waited.

The shadows disappeared. There were no sounds of heavy feet on the platform. Only the gentle huffing of the engine could be heard.

Dead silence.

A hand slammed into the round window on the door, shattering the glass. It seized the door by the sill, cutting its hand deeply, and pulled. The metal twisted and bent until it was free enough from the frame to be opened. The door was flung away from the car. Flockmocker opened his mouth to protest, but un-pocketed something sharp looking instead.

Two men stepped in, pointed at Turner and went after him – ignoring everyone else in the room.

Turner knew what they had come for, and he was only half of their mission. He backed up a few steps, giving himself room to fight – as much room as could be had in the narrow railcar.

AG fired first. He didn't miss.

A metallic twang accompanied the ricocheting bullet that hit the sideboard instead. The man looked at AG, appearing annoyed. He seized AG by the arm that held the gun, twisted, and then flung him across one of the couches.

Forrer took a step back to brace himself and raised his pistol.

Chapter 7

Residence of Professor L. Gantry, PhD Geo
Sutton, Surrey, Great Britain

Someone was watching her. Oh, my yes, it was a familiar sensation. Possibly it was the fellow from the Foreign Office. Mr. Lowell had sent him now that the Prussians had made an attempted kidnapping. It almost seemed to be a matter of courtesy that the Foreign Office spy made himself a tad obvious.

No, it wasn't him. This was someone else: one of bio-mechanical men who worked for the Frenchman, Hetzel? No, they had become bored with her and given up. Prussians. It had to be Prussians.

Or perhaps, just a messenger or footman.

Lettie glanced over at the new, yet unreleased Mark IV – Martini Henry rifle given to her as a present.

Rose entered Professor Gantry's parlor with a pot of tea and a slice of raisin bread with sweet butter, and tried not to roll her eyes at the sight of the place. At this point, Rose should have been used to the idea that Lettie rarely had visitors, beyond Miranda Gray, and that the room had been re-purposed into a study – workspace – laboratory. It was a mess of papers, maps, one large blackboard with mathematical hieroglyphs scrawled out in chalk, and rocks – far too many rocks. She was a bit embarrassed by it all, though perhaps more so for Rose's sake. Rose took pride in her domestic realm and Lettie was a whirlwind of destruction to that pristine empire.

Newer to the chaos were packages and letters. Six months after the whole business of the Earthshaker, Iceland, the Prussians, and one American, Lettie was still being inundated with praise and gifts – none of which she required or desired. Several women's development groups had taken notice and now wanted her sponsorship for their activities. Some she approved of, such as equal pay for women in the workplace. Some she wasn't sure about, such as the vote, but then should ladies receive the franchise, she'd likely be first in line to cast a ballot. Some women's issues she didn't entirely approve of, though not because she disagreed overall, but because she had no firsthand knowledge, and supporting certain marriage bills before Parliament struck her as being inappropriate. She was un-married, and not entirely disappointed that she would likely remain so for the rest of her life. At this point, marriage for the sake of starting a family was laughable. She was too old to safely have a first child – at least she was sure she'd read that somewhere. And of course, there was the lack of prospects.

A cold sensation ran down her arms and across her shoulders.

She had one prospect – a dubious one at best.

She looked over at the bookcase, groaning under the weight of the disorganized books, and saw near the top a dog-eared copy of her treatise on volcanic ash types. Stuffed inside was a TIPSY message. Sending anything through the TransAtlantic Pneumatic System was dreadfully expensive. He must have meant it. A hastily written, probably while on board a ship, message.

He asked her to marry him.

It was impossible of course.

He was a man of questionable character. Although, last year, he had climbed down into a volcanic vent to try and save her. Lettie smiled a bit. They had saved each other, realistically speaking. And he had said he loved her.

Her smile faded. She'd heard it before and each time it turned into disaster.

Staring out over her reading glasses, she picked up one rectangular package near the pot of tea Rose had set down on her desk. A heavy box, no doubt filled with dried salted cod. The return address indicated the Icelandic Fisherman's Society of Vik. One of twenty local collectives that had battled against Britain and Russia for years over fishing rights for years. Yet now, with Iceland on the verge of full independence and Lettie's substantial participation in stopping the Earthshaker from destroying the island and stopping the Prussian military, relations between the nations had improved. Oh, they were still testy, but the good will generated had not yet worn off. Thus, she received gifts of fish, dried fish, fish eggs, and something she was informed of by the post service as being too vile smelling to be allowed into the country. Fermented Shark, she was certain. Part of her was sorry she didn't get to try it – part of her knew better. A gift was a gift and she would send them a thank you note regardless.

British fishing industry representatives sent letters of thanks, boxes of much more palatable biscuits, and requests for endorsements: a mention in her next newspaper article – which she hadn't written and wasn't likely to.

There was a knock at the door, and Lettie looked up at the clock on the mantle. Eleven in the morning. It certainly wasn't a caller. Miranda perhaps, but it was a bit too early for her friend. Besides, the clutter made Miranda uneasy and thus they tended to meet at her house instead of Lettie's. In the afternoon, of course.

If it was the Prussian spy, it was too much cheek and she'd have to do something about it. She glared over confidently at the Martini Henry.

She could hear Rose answering the door. It was a telegram. Well, at least it wasn't a box of fish. She wasn't ungrateful for the honest meaning with the gifts, but it was getting to be a bit much.

Rose returned with the telegram on a tray – entirely unnecessary but Lettie knew she liked to do it. "A message, Professor. Oh, and I checked – not a soul out there this morning, beyond that fellow." Rose had made it part of her occupation to look for the rude men sent to spy on her employer.

"Thank you, Rose."

"Will you need help with all these," she couldn't find the words.

"In an hour or so. I shall have to make sure I have enough note cards and postal stamps. We may need to send out for more."

Rose shook her head at all of it, sniffed slightly at the box on Lettie's desk, and walked away quickly.

Lettie ignored the telegram for a moment. One package, very soft looking, drew her attention. In it was a scarf. It was lovely. Knitted. Home spun wool, dyed a lovely mustard yellow. The note inside said it was made by the wife of the Mayor of Hafnarfjörður. She instantly liked it. It was personal and a touch intimate.

Lettie stood up. This was a time to make decisions. She strode over to the window to look out on her pleasant neighborhood. Even her usually critical neighbors had become much less acrimonious about her single state since she'd become a celebrity. Between her experience with the eruption of Krakatoa and the business in Iceland, she'd gained a positive reputation.

She was at the height of her power and ought to put it into play.

The racially motivated riots in London would not steal her energy to teach and to learn. It would only be a matter of time before all the anger dissipated and things got back to normal, she repeated often to herself.

She ached to be in the field again. The dirt, the rocks, the sounds of rumbling under her feet. While she did enjoy teaching, she found the experience draining due to the constant administrative tasks on top of providing information.

One of the letters she kept centrally was from Professor Aronnax of the Paris National Museum of Natural History, inviting her to help them redesign their geology displays. In a world after Krakatoa, much of academia had been forced to rethink its ideas of how the earth worked. That could be a lovely challenge and she'd enjoy a trip to Paris in the off season.

Outside, a burst of wind blew curled, fallen leaves across a damp road. The green, early arrivals chased each other down the street. A footman from one of the larger houses was off on an errand, bundled up against the cold. Scattered clouds kept re-casting the light from gray to bright. She might go out today and visit Miranda, if the lady was at home. She loved her little place in Surrey, but it was time to start moving again. She hated sitting still for very long, which might also account for why the sedentary university life wasn't quite agreeing with her.

Where to go? Paris?

If not going abroad, what about Ipswich? She'd been invited to lecture by the Ipswich Geological Society. She rather liked them; a clever bunch of amateur scientists and mystery hunters.

What about a new volcano to study?

She hadn't been to the Hawaiian Islands and heard that its most active crater was being quite spectacular. Etna in Italy was being testy as usual. Where hadn't anyone been before?

Another footman, or some such occupied man, walked by, taking interest in her house. She knew he couldn't see her behind the curtains, but she could see him. He wasn't someone she recognized – not that she was an expert, but the neighborhood was not heavily populated, thus everyone knew, or knew of, everyone else.

He was taking too much of an interest.

Lord of Mercy, a new spy? He wasn't very good.

This was quite ridiculous.

As he turned slightly, she could see his short cropped hair. *Prussian*. It had to be another Prussian. Fuming, she seized the rifle and stormed out into the wind, the voice of Rose following, calling to her in a panicked pitch.

Feeling every bit the British heroine, Boudicca, with pieces of her hair whipping up in the air, her skirts billowing around her like smoke, and the rifle gleaming in the lamplight, Lettie marched after the man. "You there. Stop!"

The man stopped but did not turn around.

Damn whatever the neighbors thought, Lettie shouldered the rifle with the skill of an infantryman. "Turn around." She'd practiced for this moment.

Slowly, he did turn, stiffly. His face remained impassive and mostly shadowed.

Lettie stepped to within a yard of him – hopefully still out of his reach. She braced and kept the muzzle pointed at him. "You tell Admiral Hagan, or whomever you report to in the Prussian government, that this is my neighborhood, in my country. I will defend it, my household, and myself to the bitter last if I must. Do you understand?"

He seemed amused and confused at the same time. His face fell back into a state of non-concern.

"Tell them that the American Naval Officer and I are no longer connected in anyway, and he will not come running to my rescue if you try to use me ..."

The man held up his hand and stepped forward into better street light. The details that had been shadowed were now much clearer. A long tube stretched from his temple back over his ear and down his spine.

A bio-mechanical man.

"Madmoiselle," he said with a tingy voice. "I am here because the Prussians are. My commander has sent me to protect you. You should quiet yourself and go inside where it is safer for you." He didn't blink. "Being hysterical will not help." A plate of bronze riveted into his skull caught a glint of light. Despite all his bio-enhancements, he might well look normal in poor light. Then again, it was possible his enhancements were intended to send a message to the Prussians: leave Lettie Gantry alone, or else.

Hysterical? The common dismissal of women's anger? Lettie must have stared for a full minute, her mouth slightly open in readiness for the terse remark she desperately wanted to spit at him, before she straightened up. Never once did she lower the rifle. Her face burned in rage. She was breathing hard now and could barely speak. But speak, she would. Calmly. Aggressively. Lettie lowered her voice to a low, threatening tone. "If I see you around here again, I will shoot you as the French spy you are. And if you think I accept Monsieur Hetzel at his word that he only wishes to protect me, then you are insane. He can find another neighborhood to fight the Franco-Prussian war again."

"Very wise of you, Madame."

She eyed him closely. "An interesting answer."

"A truthful one."

She snapped the action out and back. "Then, for that, I'll give you the count of ten to get out of my sight."

"Madame ..."

"Never, ever, doubt that I can use this weapon. Don't ever make the mistake of thinking I won't. One."

He didn't wait for "two."

Behind Lettie, Rose and the gardener, Bernard, raced down the steps and into the street where Lettie was keeping her stance. Rose had a heavy, cast-iron skillet. Bernard had another rifle from Lettie's collection. Twice the height of Rose and just as wide, he was an imposing figure easily bullied by the housekeeper, but no one else. Perhaps he liked how Rose treated him or just found it amusing, Lettie thought, as she turned around to acknowledge them. Regardless, they trusted each other and she trusted them implicitly.

The bio-man continued walking down the street until they couldn't see him anymore.

"Was he one of *them*," Rose asked. "One of the fixed fellows?"

"Yes."

Bernard slowly lowered his gun but kept searching the street for movement. "Better than one o' those krauts." When Lettie laughed a little, he nodded his big head and added, "I didn' ask permission fer this." He held the rifle out. "Just thought I shouldn' show up to a gun fight with lawn trimmers."

Lettie barked out an un-resistible laugh. "Well done both of you. I don't mind that you borrowed it, Bernard. But please tell me you had the good sense to load it first?"

Bernard looked shocked that she would even ask. "Of course, ma'am."

"Well, that's good because it was smarter than me." She worked the action of the rifle several times, showing that no cartridges were being expelled.

Perhaps it would be best if she just found some remote, unheard of volcano to study and to leave everything behind for a while. The College was out of session for the summer. The timing was perfect to go find the adventure she was born to enjoy.

At the door, Rose stepped aside to allow Lettie to enter. "Oh, Professor, that telegram you got. I noticed it's from Professor Moore."

That was odd, why would he send her a telegram?

What an evening. Back inside the safety of her home, Lettie absently picked up the telegram after pouring a cup of tea and read it.

Rose was correct: it had come from Kent – from the home of her dear friend Kit Moore. She adored Kit and his "friend" William. She didn't mind their secret and was happy to keep it. It made her feel quite good thinking about the love they shared. What a shame too many others didn't.

Secret indeed. Such a secret could land one, or both of them, in prison.

Christopher Moore, Kit, was older than Lettie by about five years, and always going home to Kent to recover from city life. Perhaps he wasn't feeling well. She would have to bring him some potato and leek soup, which her well-to-do Welsh mother had sworn could cure anything. Kit had been known to feign illness just so that she would provide him with the soup.

She scanned over the brief message.

The good feelings vanished.

Chapter 8

The Flockmocker All-in-One Passenger Locomotive

Forrer didn't quite remember the actual time he was in the air, but his landing on the back of the couch and flipping over was very clear. The creatures were stronger than he'd thought. His old wound, from Hawaii the year earlier, now hurt again, as if fresh. Where was his gun?

He stood up, ready to fight.

AG was slumped against the wall near the doorway, and the two monsters were joining forces against Turner.

That was when Forrer got a good look at the men – the creatures. Neither had the look of a human being in control of his faculties. They scowled and remained unblinking for long, unnatural periods of time. Both had shaved heads with perhaps a week's worth of hair growth. Their skin was blotchy and gray, as though decomposing corpses. Tubes were shoved under their skin, leaving horrifying scars and barely-healed flesh at the points of connection. Nothing remotely compassionate lingered in their eyes. They looked like convicts who'd died a year before.

"Hey!" he called out, alerting them that Turner was not alone.

The monster closest to Forrer turned without hesitation and advanced on the Lieutenant.

Turner's man reached out to seize him, but Turner ducked away, then slammed his fist into the creature's side. Turner darted left, confusing his attacker, and punched him in the kidney. Knowing his predator, Turner got out of reach immediately.

It was a good lesson for Forrer, who did his all to both dodge attack and look for his weapon.

He spotted it.

Turner's monster suddenly caught Turner by the arm, and with no interest in the blows and kicks he was receiving, began dragging Turner toward the door. It wasn't just an attack! It was a kidnapping! It was looking around on the floor too. A moment later, it saw what it was looking for: the relic. Turner's fight was keeping the monster from picking up the object, but that would only last for so long.

Forrer dropped to the floor and rolled to where his gun had landed, under the couch. He could see the gun. He could almost reach it.

The creature behind him grabbed his leg and pulled him out of reach of his gun. Forrer rolled over and kicked hard at the creature's face. His leg freed, he pushed away from the temporarily confused monster and dove again for the gun.

First shot was supposed to drop Turner's abductor. It slowed him, but did not stop him. It reached down finally and seized the relic off the floor. Forrer had three more shots. Two shattered the cranium of the monster and it let go of Turner. Wobbling, shaking, clutching the object, showing no emotion on its face, the creature at last flopped on the floor for a few seconds. The relic landed with a loud cracking noise quickly buried under the body.

Forrer's leg was snatched up and he was dragged back so violently, he dropped the weapon again. He heard Turner shouting. The creature let go of his leg and gripped him by the throat. Lifted up to where his feet no longer touched the ground, Forrer began flailing and kicking.

A bullet burst through the creature's forehead and out the back.

It didn't stop. It kept choking him.

The gun was slammed straight into its face, with no effect.

Turner jumped on its back and began yanking its head up. It let go of Forrer and spun around to try to toss Turner off its back.

"Outta the way!" Flockmocker screamed.

Turner let go and landed a foot away from Forrer.

Flockmocker slammed the hand-crank generator onto the floor and aimed the weapon at the creature's chest. A bolt of lightning shattered the air between the Professor and the creature. Flockmocker was knocked down, hard by the energy.

Forrer remembered little else but that a charred heap of ash was all that lay near his feet. The brief lack of oxygen made his head ache – burn in fact. Turner didn't look too good but happily alive. AG was even stirring and mumbling something about how long it had taken Flockmocker to respond.

"That," Turner began, "Is that the same thing you used on the *Albatross*, in the Indies?"

"Modified," Flockmocker crowed with pride.

"Of course. Isn't everything?" Turner put his hand on Forrer's shoulder. "Are you alright?"

"Define 'alright.'" Forrer didn't want to move.

"Professor, my apologies, for the – the …" Turner looked around the room.

"Eh!" was all that he got in response, as if a combination of "who cares" and "as if you could do anything about it."

"You were asking 'what if,' weren't you sir? I think this answers a bit, don't you?" Forrer said, holding his head. "Somebody wants the object – and you!"

Turner rubbed his arm. "Why me?" he half whispered.

"You're joking, sir. Right? Hetzel has been after you for a long time."

Shaking his head, he pointed to the chair for Forrer to sit down before he fell down. "We'd achieved a truce. He wouldn't bother me if I didn't tell the whole world about him."

Forrer began rubbing the painful bruising around his neck and looking at a handkerchief to see if he was bleeding. "He probably assumes you told the Old Men, maybe the Navy, and is after you." His throat was tight. For a brief second, he wondered if he knew better now what Turner had felt during his failed hanging? He wouldn't ask.

Turner didn't believe it. "It's been a year. If I was going to make a public statement, I would have, and Hetzel's jig would be up. The Old Men and the War Department both already know about him. I'm not the threat he's worried about."

Flockmocker looked down at the bullet-riddled creature, laying on the floor, near the now-missing door. "These are Hetzel's men. Look at 'em. They're crude, but carefully enhanced. Say what you will about the process, but Hetzel's doctors kept things nice and tidy whenever possible. This looks like it was rushed a bit."

Turner could only nod in agreement.

AG stretched his back, perhaps to free it from stiffness and pain, but clearly to no avail. He looked stiff and hurt. "Could it be someone other than Hetzel? Who in God's name would have bio-men like those?"

It seemed that Turner couldn't even shake his head to disagree now. "There's something wrong here and that object, under there, is part of it. It's just a hunch, but I think we have more than one entity making these … We need more information." He began trying to move the body of one of the monsters with his foot.

"We need to get that thing locked up safely," AG stated, by the sound of his voice, not allowing for any refusal. "Far from here. There's no back up out here."

Forrer looked up, "As we seem to be the only back up, I must agree. Sir," he looked to Turner, "this is your call. What do you want us to do?"

"Take care of your injuries, for now."

Forrer nodded properly, knowing it was an order as much as a recommendation. He knew Turner would be lost in his own thoughts for a while, until he could come up with a plan. Forrer honestly wished he could know what his friend and commander was thinking.

Pulling on the base of the object, it was soon clear that the thing had broken into two parts.

Turner picked up the relic pieces and walked away to the far side of the compartment.

Forrer wanted to know what was going through his head. Turner kept staring at the object, then announced he had an idea – a bad idea – a bad idea that could backfire and do irreparable damage to a relationship that had suffered enough …

"No, I can't do that. Not after all I've already done to her."

Slamming the object down on to the couch next to Forrer, probably wanting more than ever to throw it out the now exposed passenger exit, he looked at his temporary party.

Forrer tried not nursing his neck injury that would probably bruise deeply more than anything. He didn't want Turner worrying.

Flockmocker finally removed himself from staring at the one, whole creature, appearing to be annoyed but not damaged.

AG, who keep rubbing his wrist and his arm, and sporting a dramatic slice across his forehead. Forrer easily guessed that AG didn't feel so good himself, especially around his ribs.

Turner suddenly commanded, "AG, turn this bucket around. We need to get to New York – now."

"We may lose a little speed due to drag from that missing door, but not too much. Two days?"

"That long?"

"We can't fly this thing."

Turner let his lopsided smile speak his mind, like he always did, Forrer noted.

"Perhaps I can help with that," Turner said. When AG returned his comment with a smile and a raised eyebrow, he demanded solidly, "How quickly can we get moving?"

The engineer didn't argue or hesitate. "On route, ten minutes." AG stepped through the doorway onto the platform and began shouting for the station manager. In a moment, the two men were arguing until AG showed them some sort of badge. The argument ended and AG nodded to the men inside the railcar. "Five minutes. We have priority to the turntable." Still rubbing his wrist, he headed off toward the engine.

In a pitiable moment, Flockmocker held up a tooth. "Well, it needed to go anyway. Was botherin' the hell out of me. I was hoping to use my new …" He didn't bother to elaborate. "Lock down what you don't want falling on you. Bandages in the cabinet." He spit some blood from the extraction in his mouth. "I have a sample to test."

Forrer and Turner were left in the car alone, searching desperately for anything that needed to be secured before the train left the station. The Lieutenant gathered up his papers and case, Turner snagged his belongings and the object, and they relocated far away from the open doorway.

"Sir, what is sticking out of that piece?" Forrer pointed to the couch.

Turner looked and realized that the broken relic had been hollow. Old paper – perhaps papyrus – protruded from the obelisk section. It was several sheets, tightly rolled. As he started to unroll it, a sound much like breaking bread crusts made him stop. The pages were too old. If he did any more, they could shatter.

He held perfectly still, with the pages slightly revealed.

Schematics. If what little he could see was true for the rest of the document, it was a set of plans for bio-mechanics. Not only did the statue provide instruction on how to make a bio-mechanical person, but there was more – far more. How was that even possible?

"To the Old Men?"

Turner nodded and slowly, carefully, allowed the document to roll up again. "We have to. This is beyond anything …" He wasn't sure how to finish his sentence.

"Are they all in New York?"

His reply to the Lieutenant was an exhausted nod, then a furrowed brow. "Not the former President." His voice was sad. "He's up state, at home. Declining fast." He looked at Forrer, genuinely worried what was going through the young man's mind.

As though he heard Turner's unspoken concern, he replied, "Has it ever been easier – in the past – or is that an illusion we all cling to?"

"Perhaps."

"Riots in the streets of London, the capital of the empire that claims to be the height of human civilization. A New Confederacy gaining momentum here, at home. The number of madmen willing to destroy the world if they can't conquer it. Inventions that make automatons out of men. Please don't take this the wrong way, but sometimes I wonder if anything we do will stop all that and give us back what we think we used to have."

Turner couldn't help smiling. "We said the same thing during the War. But going backward is never an option. Too many mistakes. If there hadn't been, we wouldn't have changed in the first place." He sat down as the train jerked violently forward, just as AG had warned them. "We do make a difference, if that's what you're thinking. Small, singular, determined. Yes, even two men with a good cause can make the difference."

Neither said anything for a long time, but clung to their seats until the train settled onto the turntable and braked.

"You know, sir, I haven't met the membership of the Old Men."

"Well," Turner was happy to provide some good news. "That's about to change too."

Chapter 9

Moore Estate
County Kent, Great Britain

"You were sacked," William Smythe said with as much venom as he could muster. "Because of me. Because of us." He'd let go of Kit's hand and began to pace with the disgust of a caged animal. His long legs tended to get him around the room faster than anyone else might. Occasionally he pushed back locks of long blond hair from his face. His appearance tended to be that of an eccentric artist.

His companion was a number of years older, thin in the scalp, neat in the beard, and quite tall. Professor Christopher Moore, Kit to his friends, was an elegant gentleman with superb connections and potential, with one glaring exception.

"I was encouraged to resign before things became uncomfortable for the school." Kit was trying his best to be calm, but the truth was clear on his face – and she could see it.

Lettie took a moment to breathe, steady her nerves, and to respond. She fidgeted with her glasses until finally putting them in her jacket pocket, before she accidentally broke them. There wasn't a great deal she could say. Kit was clearly still in shock and William, bless him, was fuming. Rightfully so.

She had been raised to think of their love as something vile, unnatural, and forbidden. But sitting there, and all the time before when she'd been near them, she knew deep inside it had been a lie. Why, she didn't understand. She knew there were specific Biblical rules against two men loving one another beyond friendship, but then those rules were listed along with demands to not eat certain food, not to plant certain crops in certain ways, and to not wear clothes of mixed fibers. Those rules turned out to be nonsense in the modern era, why couldn't that remaining mandate be ignored too? She hated feeling naïve, but she hated imagining what Kit and William were going through even more. She turned her focus back to them.

Not having an income was unlikely to harm Kit in any substantial way. The Moore family had plenty of money and land. He would not suffer starvation or deprivation, in the material sense. She suspected that the Moores were aware of Kit's unique nature and had chosen familial love over religious duty. William's family, the Smythe's, were blissfully ignorant and no one was attempting to change that.

Yet money wasn't everything, as the saying went. Kit was now forced to live under a shared roof – albeit a pleasant and relatively tolerant one. And he was stuck in the country, which had the dreadful habit of being far more conservative than was necessary. Few people meant that everyone was caught up in each other's business – something not healthy for Kit.

The loss of his position also caused him to become dependent, which the aging gentleman was horrified to consider. On his own, independent, and in the crowded city, he could live according to his own rules. William could come and go, and rarely would anyone either care or notice.

At least, no one cared or noticed until the Earthshaker had started is ravings in the newspapers. She had to wonder if all the hatred that had been stirred up and brought to the surface would have simple died of neglect had the Shaker not made casual hatred seem reasonable.

"Now what," William demanded.

"We wait." Kit hadn't meant to sound cross; it wasn't his way. "We wait until things calm down and better minds are in charge."

"They sacked you based on a rumor!"

Kit took a deep breath before replying, "I was forced to resign. And yes, because some horrible preacher, or whatever he is, made it his mission in life to get even with me for some slight I never gave him."

"Just how long are we supposed to wait? We're told to be patient, but it's been hundreds of years. We're told it will be fine if only we behave in a way that lets *them* feel comfortable. I don't care if they're comfortable – it's not my purpose in life to make them comfortable – I want to live my life without their judgment and interference. Now some nobody has attacked us because he's small minded and stupid and hateful – and I'm the one who must be patient?"

"It made him feel important," Lettie finally added. "Now he's shown the world he has control over those who used to appear to have control over him. He got his victory. It will never matter to him that it was true or not; important or not; his business or not. He was looking for someone to harm so that he could feel big in a world that made him otherwise feel small."

William stopped pacing and glared at her. "Rather cold of you, dear."

"Logical. I try to see things rationally. And, as I am not directly affected by this – though it is painful to see two men I adore dearly being unfairly harmed – I am trying to offer the cool voice of logic. You two are those being hurt – if you are emotional, no person on this Earth has the right to deny you that." She couldn't look at William. "I honestly don't know what else to do." Crying or yelling wouldn't help – besides, such a response was really only appropriate from Kit or William.

His hand was cold but offered with such kindness, she would not reject it. William knelt in front of her. "I suppose, dear, it wouldn't be fair to expect anything less than that from such a good scientist. And friend."

Kit's hand was on top of theirs an instant later.

"What now?" she asked Kit.

"I think I should like to travel? I haven't been to see my friends in Amsterdam in a while. There's also a dig going on near the Black Sea. A former colleague says he's found signs of ancient settlements there. Seems ancient peoples got about far more than we thought. I think I might …"

The knock on the front door was moderately loud, but then everything in the country seemed to be pronounced. Out of habit, they separated from one another, stopped talking, and arranged themselves to present a picture of British society should it be a caller arriving.

The door was opened and the low, standard discussion between the visitor and the footman commenced. Actual words were not discernable. For the noises in the hallway, the caller was asked to wait. A moment later the footman entered the parlor. "Excuse me, sir. But there is a gentleman who wishes – who wishes a moment with

Professor Gantry." His eyes looked immediately to her. After receiving a nod from Kit, the footman walked over to Lettie and presented a calling card on a tray.

"I don't know that I told anyone, except Miranda Gray, that I was coming out to see you." She lifted the card to see the clean typeface printing on it. Lettie shut her eyes, as if to hide that fact that she was rolling them. "Thank you. Kit, may I borrow the library for a moment?"

"Of course. Is this something …" Kit looked from Lettie to William and back.

"No, no! I will only be a moment."

The footman stood up. "With your permission sir, I'll ask the gentleman to wait in the library. Should I ask the maid to bring …"

"No." Lettie said, before Kit could reply. "No tea. He will not be staying that long."

Kit agreed with some hesitation. Lettie was prone to getting strange visitors and even stranger demands – but rarely someone who would follow her to Kent.

After the footman left the room, William couldn't help himself by asking, "Is it your American? Did he track you up here like a buffalo or whatever Americans track?"

Lettie looked a bit surprised. She hadn't thought of that, but no. It wasn't Tom Turner. "A bit of business, that's all. I'll be right back."

She left the two distressed gentlemen in the parlor and quietly slipped into the library. The room was darker and colder as it had not been made up for visitors. The footman had hastily opened the curtains to make it somewhat acceptable. It had the flavor of an old-fashioned den – perhaps from the turn of the century. Never dusty, but always a little stale from the slow decay of paper.

Harcourt K. Lowell, of the Foreign Office, was standing in anticipation of her presence and holding his hat – something that indicated that he had no intention of staying very long. He looked precisely the same as the last time she'd seen him – right down to the same bland but excellent suit, conservative watch chain and fob, beaver hat, and fine kid gloves. Dark eyes and slick black hair completed the appearance of a businessman – yet he wasn't.

"Mr. Lowell. Good day. You've come a long way out for brief visit."

"Professor. I don't really like the country but this is important."

"Please sit down," she then indicated a comfortable chair opposite the one she would choose. "What in heaven's name would drag you out so far from the city?"

"I journeyed all the way to Iceland to meet you."

"In a city. With a British embassy."

"Touché." He sat down, keeping his hat on his lap. "Ah – before we begin, are your two colleagues out of the range of hearing?"

Her hackles went up. "They are both good men, and not in the habit of listening in …"

Lowell's hand went up. "What I have to say is of national importance and I simply want to know that our conversation is private. I know the – circumstances – around which Professor Moore is here and not in London …"

Her eyes grew wide.

"… And I honestly think it's no business of the Foreign Office if they are not committing acts of treason."

She relaxed.

"I will not make a statement about things I think are best left quiet and under the proviso that they are no one's business."

"Very liberal of you."

"A Tory in practice, a Whig at heart." He shifted in his seat, as though what he was there for was far more uncomfortable. "I'll be blunt."

"A good practice between us."

He smiled. "Have you had any communication from Commander Thomas Turner?"

Ouch. "A few months ago, a TIPSY letter, but nothing since."

"No package or set of drawings?"

"No, none at all. Is that really why I was harassed by the Prussians? I was under the impression they want to use me for leverage."

"We have officially dissuaded them from the notion. Turns out they want our support in resisting German unification. How ironic, when think about it. Have you noticed any of them around?"

"Not for a while. There was some fellow but not Prussian."

"French," Lowell asked knowingly.

"*Oui.*" She shifted nervously. Now what? Am I supposed to receive something from someone? I have yet to, or, not that I am aware of."

Lowell scowled. "I rather wish you had and simply forgotten to notify me. That would be considerably easier."

"Have I done something wrong?"

He looked up, realizing he'd failed to take her point of view into account. "My apologies, Professor. You have not done anything wrong. In fact, your accomplishments and actions in Iceland are still having a positive impact. I cannot go into excessive detail."

Lettie smiled and shook her head. "I daresay, you rarely can. Tell me what is allowable and I will, as ever, attempt to help."

He stood up abruptly. "There's nothing you need worry about. I would only ask that you keep a watchful eye out for any unusual packages that come for your attention in the next few months."

That was oddly put, she thought. "I will do so, though you may want to identify 'unusual' a tad more clearly. I have thus far received packages of both dried and barely dead codfish, as gifts of appreciation. Two gold watches, the significance of which eludes me. Handkerchiefs by the dozens, several quite lovely ones. Letters of thanks. And the occasional notice of disapproval that I ruined someone's chance at stealing fishing rights, threatened their sense of the Universe, blah, blah, blah."

"Your almost usual mail. Any real threats?" he asked genuinely.

"None. Even those complaining about my disregard for a natural woman's place seem to keep a civil tongue in their heads. No threats at this time."

"You're luckier than the Foreign Secretary. I will not give you all the horrible things sent to him."

"I have an imagination – I can believe it. Civil disagreement and discourse seem to be lacking in the public these days. I consider myself lucky so far."

Lowell nodded, looking possibly for an exit. He'd wasted his time coming out to the Kent countryside. "Mr. Turner has the strangest luck, and we suspect that he found something he should not have. An accidental mismanagement of evidence. Perhaps."

Lettie did not rise, and thus did not allow Lowell to take his leave. After a moment, she gazed up at him. "Does it have anything to do with those stories coming from America, about a strange vessel attacking towns? Yes, I have read about them in the papers."

"No, but I do think Commander Turner may get involved in that nasty business too. I do wish the Americans would take care of real issues instead of making up goblins in the night."

"As we do?" Lettie allowed the question to sink in. "I daresay I am here because the Shaker gave permission to goblin-makers here in our empire. And they're running amok on the streets of London."

He sat down again. "Have you considered travelling for a bit? Getting away from all this? It can't be easy for you." The tone of his voice was surprising.

"It's hardly easy for anyone of decency. Weren't you just last month telling me to stay put?"

"Things have changed. Yet, as a public figure, which you are now if not before, you are a potential target. The Foreign Secretary has security around him. The Ministers are protected. There are guards for Her Majesty. But for the average lady?"

"I carry the pistol, as you recommended."

"I think more needs to be done. Time away from the limelight."

"I might go up to Ipswich. I've been offered the honorary position of President *in Abstentia* of the Ipswich Geological Society."

Lowell held back a slight chuckle.

Sighing, she looked at him squarely. "I have been thinking about going back into the field. It is where I am happiest and can do the most good. With the change in circumstance for Professor Moore complete, I must say that I do not expect to be far behind in losing my positon at the College. Forcing the Professor's resignation has likely emboldened some of the leadership."

"They won't dismiss you; you're too popular and, if I may say, too circumspect in your living."

"No, they won't dare dismiss me, but they will – and are already – making life at the College quite unbearable. The Dean would like nothing more than my resignation. I enjoy teaching. Lord knows I'm quite comfortable with the sound of my own voice," she laughed. "But I belong in the dirt, up to my elbows in mud and lava. It is very likely I'll look to travel abroad."

This time Lowell stood up and made his way to the door. Lettie went with him. "If you require anything, Professor, you know it would be my pleasure to assist you."

"Getting easy travel papers would be a relief."

"Consider it done."

"And please, Mr. Lowell, don't worry about unusual packages. Should I receive one, which I doubt I will, I will inform you right away. If I am out of the country, I will instruct my staff to do exactly that."

They walked quietly to the door – no need to disturb the footman.

"Thank you Professor."

"I'm sorry your trip was for nothing, Mr. Lowell."

"Not for nothing. I had a delightful chat with you and received assurances that relieve any anxiety I may have had. Very well worth …"

He stopped mid-stride and sentence, held up his hand, and closed the door slightly. Lowell looked outside, his body showing alarm. Suddenly he pulled open the door and took four large steps out.

"Mr. Lowell, what is it? Is there someone out there?"

"I think there was." Lowell turned to her and fiercely stated, "Professor, it is time you took up residence outside of England. Far outside of England."

"I feel exiled. Are you going to tell me why?"

"I think you know." He put his hat on his head, not bothering to adjust it, and began scanning the far gate, carriage house, and field with a shocking intensity. "Travel in company, keep low in the public sphere, and pick your next volcano. Tell no one but me where you're going."

"Impossible. There are too many people who I'll need help from – my staff – contacts abroad …"

"Then limit whom you tell to only the smallest number. Pick a place and I will arrange anything you need."

Lettie stopped him by his elbow. "This is really about Commander Turner?"

"I think it's about far, far more than one man."

Lowell walked away, constantly looking about.

How had he gotten to the Moores without a carriage? She stayed transfixed on the porch for so long, both Kit and William came out to check on her.

"What does he want? Who was he?" Kit held out a cup of tea to her.

She didn't take it. "Foreign Office."

Kit held his breath and William sat down – hard.

"Gentlemen," she said with much official tone. "I have a feeling I'm going to need your assistance. I cannot tell you why, because I'm not allowed to. I have nothing yet to tell anyway. But if my suspicion is correct, I will need you to help me for no better reason than it serves your country and humanity. And you'd have every right to turn away, considering how your country and so-called humanity have treated you."

Kit edged closer to her and insisted she take the cup. "But for you – anything."

"Besides," added William, "it's our world too. What do you think you may need? Eventually?"

Chapter 10

Near Central Park – South
New York, New York, United States of America

The Mercer Hotel was all posh and had an enviable address. If one was to stay anywhere temporarily, this was the place. If one was to move in with the intention of leaving but never actually go, this was still the place.

The exterior of the building was white marble, chiseled into a dramatic Federalist design of Roman columns, cap stones, and imperious, toga-clad figures in classic poses. The windows were large rectangles of excellent glass shrouded with layers of exquisite velvet and linen curtains.

Inside the floors were rich, polished, dark wood covered liberally with expensive Persian rugs. Mirrors, desks, electric lights, and the strange ringing of a newly installed telephone device made it as modern as it was opulent.

No wonder Mrs. Sherman insisted their New York residence be the Mercer. Mr. Sherman was convinced it was for the modern comforts in an elegant setting that pleased her. According to Mrs. Sherman, she was glad that the staff could keep an eye on her trouble-attracting husband while providing him with the gentle lifestyle she felt he'd earned.

The Chief Clerk nudged his assistant and pointed toward the woman in silhouette exiting the lobby. By her outline, for they simply could not make out any details of her person with the back drop of bright sunlight streaming in the front door, she was dressed to promenade. Her shape was one of a well-tailored lady, with an acceptably fashionable bustle, short walking length skirts, furred coat and muff. A tall hat sat well-pinned to her curly, supremely well-coifed hair.

It was at that moment he realized he'd never actually seen the lady in question. By her stride and command of the lobby, it was no doubt Mrs. Sherman, wife of the famous general. Very independent but then, generals usually didn't need wives around to pester them. Still – he hadn't actually seen her face. Not ever. He had no idea what color hair or eyes she had. For a woman married to a 63-year old man, and supposedly not too much younger, she had the build of a girl, with a slender waist that adjusted to the latest shape in corsets with ease. Her motions and gestures were free of swollen joints and shriveling bones.

To his surprise, she returned with two naval officers, as though she'd met them on her way out and turned around immediately. She was chatting with them and paying no mind to the staff chaos around her.

Well that was maddening; the officers were a bit taller than she, and blocked his view. Red hair. Ah. He did see that much. A head full of rich, mahogany curls at the forehead and smooth coils lifting her hair to pile up under her hat.

No older woman had that hair – she must truly be much younger than the general. Well – good for him. He'd lost one wife during the war, it suited him to have found a stylish lady of youthful energy to keep his fading days full of interest.

As if she had heard his thoughts, she stared at him over the shoulder of the higher-ranking officer. The Chief Clerk turned his attention to his papers, unnecessarily shuffling them.

The three-some used the elevator and disappeared upward to the top floor.

Turner and Forrer were both incredibly intrigued to finally meet the elusive Mrs. Sherman. She walked quickly from the elevator and signaled them to follow. Her key was out and the door to the suite gave her no trouble at all. She stopped inside the door frame and called out, "Cump? The gentlemen are here."

General, now retired and very relieved to be so, William Tecumseh Sherman came out of one of the side rooms with a book in his hands and a small caliber pistol laying across the open pages. His hair was as unkempt as ever but it did appear he'd attempted to comb it into place. White and pale red strands stood up in one or two places, especially where they had been cut short. His hazel eyes were alert. Once he'd seen who had come in, he stood up straight, revealing that he was not a tottering old fellow but a tall, thin man with some energy to him still. His beard had gone completely white, and it was a wonder that the rest of him hadn't too – with all that was going on. Before any comment could be made about it, he slipped the pistol into his pocket and energetically stuck out his hand to Turner.

"Good to see you again, son."

"Thank you, sir. Mrs. Sherman was gracious enough to escort us up."

Sherman turned toward his wife, who was already shedding her coat and unpinning her hat. "Given up shopping today?"

She looked up at the men watching her and replied, "What could I possibly buy that would make up for losing this moment?" She set the hat on the piano, a most uncivilized place to leave such a chapeau.

Turner looked quickly around the apartments. There was no sign of a live-in maid or butler. Odd bits of clothing had been set in places, such as a pair of gloves on the dining table and a top hat on the book case. It seemed the General had not changed his untidy habits from the war years and Mrs. Sherman had not insisted he should. Things were not painfully neat – certainly not sterile – yet it was a clean, lived-in, and bright place.

For the first time since he'd heard of her in the news, or heard mention of her by the Old Men, he was face to face with Mrs. Sherman.

"Ma'am, with your permission, I'd like to introduce my colleague." Even with a general in the room, the introduction went to the lady first.

"By all means. I've been nattering at you two since I found you floundering on the hotel steps, but we certainly haven't been introduced."

Turner nodded and gestured to the very excited but well-behaved Forrer. "Ma'am, General, this is Lieutenant Albert Forrer. An officer I'd be lost without."

In an instant, Forrer's cheeks flushed a little. Turner was always gracious, by intention, and perhaps he'd been too much so this time. Yet, Forrer deserved the compliment.

Both Shermans stepped forward to offer their hands. Mrs. Sherman grinned and took note of Turner. *Yes, there's the scar* but he neither needed her reminding him of it nor staring at it. "Mr. Turner, I feel as though you and I were long ago introduced."

She was a handsome woman. With a strong handshake, too. Large chocolate brown eyes and rosy skin that glowed in the well-lit suite. A direct stare that made him feel he was being peeled back like an onion. She was a bit shorter than he, but very straight in her posture, which he decided was due less to her corset and more to her confident mindset.

"Pardon me for a moment."

He thoroughly expected, from experience, that she would go to another room to allow the military men to talk. He knew that the married ladies were part and parcel with the Old Men, but he learned better when she stepped over to the piano to finish setting aside her outdoor gear. To his surprise, she tugged a little at her chignon, set high on her head, and removed something metal that could be interwoven into her fingers – to protect them or to give them greater impact should she …

Heaven forbid that the rumors were true, but it appeared that Mrs. Sherman lived up to her reputation as being quick to action – most especially when it came to her husband. Turner couldn't help the thought, but it popped into his head unbidden; the General had married his bodyguard. They had met in the War.

Well, it was no business of his to judge or comment. From the look on Forrer's face, Albert was thinking the exact same thing.

"Let's see it," the General commanded, indicating that the two officers should make themselves comfortable in the parlor.

Forrer pulled the package out of his coat and began unwinding it. It wasn't big, but it was ridiculously well wrapped in different materials. Both pieces were there.

"You seem to have broken it," Mrs. Sherman said wryly.

Turner cleared his throat, a little out of embarrassment. "Sir, have you ever seen any of Hetzel's men?"

"The bio-mechanicals? No. But I recall a description you gave me. Terrifying business."

Forrer removed the last bandage from the object and handed it to Turner, who held it out for the Sherman's to see.

"It looks ancient. But those tubes? That's not something you see," Mrs. Sherman commented.

Her husband sat very still. "Is that what one looks like when – when one's been enhanced?" Turner nodded to him. "Christ. Is this somebody's idea of joke?"

Turner handed it to Mrs. Sherman when she held out her hands. "It's no joke. Not every enhanced soldier in Hetzel's private army has tubes sticking out of him like that. Most, but not all. Hydraulic fluids are pumped through those, since of course, you cannot use the existing network of veins and arteries. If you look here, along the arm and leg, the artist who created this has suggested metal plates."

"So this could be an automaton and not necessarily a bio-mechanical human?" She realized it was an odd thing to say, considering the object had the head of an animal on the body of a human. And tubes …

"Perhaps. But it looks too much like one of Hetzel's men."

"Don't worry, dear," Sherman said playfully to his wife. "He isn't in the habit of enhancing women."

"I've never been so glad for discrimination," she retorted. "This is monstrous. How has he gotten away with it?"

Forrer spoke up. "If I may, I think because he serves a purpose. Like the existence of the Old Men, the official government tends to look the other way so long as it protects the nation. We may not agree, but Monsieur Hetzel is acting as a patriot. All reports show that he is extremely protective of France and French interests abroad. I do not seek to excuse this violation of humanity, or at least that's how I see it, but I believe he is convinced he is acting with a great deal of honor – for his country."

Turner felt rather proud of his colleague. It was a fair assessment. His own feelings were so mixed that he might well have presented the argument with too much bias. Forrer had only seen Hetzel's men once and was a bit less inclined toward anger. "I agree."

"So," she said, handing back the object, "you feel the attack on your train – yes, I'm aware of that – was to get ahold of this. And this represents some sort of threat to France? Or to Hetzel's army in particular?"

"Yes ma'am."

"Have you considered that it might be less of a threat and more of an opportunity?"

That wasn't something Turner had considered.

"As much as this appears to be quite ancient, we would need to do at least a metallurgical test to see what type of bronze this is – and if the recipe for the mixture contains new elements or is a pure bronze as used in ancient times." She sat down. "One way or another, what if this is more of a map or a schematic as to how bio-mechanics can be done?"

Sherman nodded in full approval. "A threat one way or another – I'm grateful it's in our hands and not his." He stretched out his long legs. "I'm sure this thing is newly minted."

Turner didn't agree, but said nothing.

"And it's awful small to be an effective schematic."

"I think it's part of something bigger, sir." He slid the document out of the obelisk. "I almost broke this too. This is very delicate. It will need an archaeologist to work with it. Too much handling and I'm convinced it will shatter."

"An important piece of a puzzle?"

"I don't know sir. But I do know that if there are more pieces, we'll need to go get them. Following the chain of events where our would-be bank robbers likely found this – stole it – we know it came out of Northern California."

Sherman scowled. "Well, that proves its newly minted. No ancient statues up in that area. Anywhere specific?"

"They seem to have picked it up from another robbery in a town called Yreka. It's near …" Turner began to notice the look of alarm on the Shermans' faces. "Near Mount Shasta."

Mr. and Mrs. Sherman exchanged glances and she pulled over a chair and sat down – before Forrer could react and fetch the chair for her.

"How up to date are you gentlemen regarding the remote town attacks?"

"Not enough I'm willing to bet, ma'am."

She looked to her husband. He stood up and brought back a map of the United States. There were red marks on it. Rolling it out for everyone to see, Sherman began on the east coast, pointing to a mark in North Carolina. "Blueridge Mountains. The Great. Eyrie. First, people started seeing lights and thought it was a volcano. We knew better. But there was some ground shaking and strange weather occurrences. Government sent a Federal Policeman to go investigate. He found remnants of some sort of laboratory and facility – mostly destroyed. And discovered that a reclusive fellow from the hills had disappeared. A body showed up a week later, in the river, so decomposed that there was not telling what killed him."

He pointed up to Illinois. "Normal, Illinois. They're building a big university there: heavy on medicine and physics. Suddenly, lights and ground shaking. Reports of a vehicle no one ever sees. A research library burned to the ground. And another fellow gone, only to be found with enough holes in him to make locals think he got chewed on before ending up in the river."

"Holes?"

"Missing parts and outright holes." He then moved to Kansas, Colorado, then Arizona, finally California. Each time, some sort of educational or research facility was destroyed and men killed.

"More holes?"

"Yes. If it was just one, I'd say some wolf or coyote got to him, but it's too common regardless of location. Different critters in these areas."

Turner noted that the path of destruction was moving west. "Seems to be on either a rail line or trail."

"That's what we thought until we noticed that the destruction seemed to move back out – as though mountain passes weren't a bother to whomever is doing this. They struck in New Mexico territory one day and were scaring the folks in California the next."

Mrs. Sherman leaned forward on her arms. "We looked at this by date, and it appears distance isn't a hindrance, so I do believe they can go anywhere. One day, halfway across the country, the next day, back at the mountain. The business at Mount Shasta is quite active, with two distinct differences from these other attacks. First, no one has disappeared nor has any facility been wrecked. There simply isn't anything there. All the other sites had either a university, some sort of school, or someone of note.

"A jealous mad scientist?" Forrer asked, knowing that as absurd as the question sounded, it was a fair question.

"I would say yes," she stated. "If not Hetzel, that is."

"What is the second difference, ma'am?" Turner asked.

"Frequency. All the attacks happened once and only once. But the activity at Shasta is continual. My thinking says that's their new base. They moved it out of North Carolina when their targets tended to be more westerly."

"Gentlemen," Sherman sat up. "The attack on your train appears to be by the same entity. Which means he can get from California to St. Louis and back in a matter of a few days."

Turner shook his head. "This isn't all Hetzel's doing. I know how the man operates. He's direct. He isn't obvious, but he his direct. The attack on our train was quite definitely by Hetzel's men. We saw them, we fought them. No question. Attacking remote towns all over the United States and being rather blatant about where his base of operations is located? That's too sloppy for Hetzel. It would also put his country at risk – the diplomatic ramifications are extreme."

Resting his head on his hands, elbows on his knees, Forrer closed his eyes for a moment. "Two parties after the same thing. If I may say so, that thing," he pointed at the relic, "needs to be far from us, without either party realizing we've hidden it."

Mrs. Sherman took back the object and weighed it in her hands. "It's heavy …" She stopped for a moment and added, "Sounds as though the porter is outside. My word he's clumsy. As I was saying, it is heavy but perhaps not too?"

He noticed Mrs. Sherman looking angrily at their door as the porter stomped up and down the corridor. The Trans-Atlantic Pneumatic System, the TIPSY? Turner thought about that. He'd used the TIPSY more than once. Expensive, but he doubted funds would be a problem in that moment. Who would they send it to?

Professor Aronnax, the sometime colleague of Captain Nemo and Professor Gantry? No. He was a smart fellow, but an academic who had little knowledge of the world. He was in the middle of France, giving Hetzel a better chance at it. Also, if the Prussians wanted to march into Paris again, as they were often threatening to do, the object could end up with any number of dangerous people, including Prussian Admiral Hagan. That thought caused a sharp shiver to run down his spine.

There was only one place it could go. The choice was obvious, but they needed to be careful to provide enough decoys and red herrings.

"I know where this must go. I'll get it to *her*."

"Won't someone guess?"

"Not if they think I still have it. By the time they think otherwise, she'll have it hidden."

It was Forrer who looked up. "I'll take the wrapping, and make a decoy – then act as one. Let them think I have it."

Sherman held up his hand. "I agree, Lieutenant, you need to take it, but the real thing. You will take it to the TIPSY. There's markings on the bandages, so those will need to go too. The rest of us *fellows*," he said, emphasizing the word to his wife, "will take decoy packages and distract whoever is watching."

"I don't like being left out. You, Mr. Sherman, and I, will take a decoy object. We do things together in such circumstances. Changing our routines would be a signal that something is not as it seems."

He was about to complain when the porter outside smashed something delicate – it sounded like pottery. "What in the hell is going on out there." He stood up only to be pulled aside by his wife.

"Cump, that's someone else out there." She turned to the officers. "Gentlemen, out! All of us!"

Three men burst through the door, spraying splinters across the carpet. Dressed in dungarees and sporting a variety of ugly enhancements, they stopped to assess the situation in the room.

The place was empty. Only just a minute before, they heard voices inside. Now the bright room was devoid of life. A breeze from the open windows caused the curtains to billow and move.

A door in the hallway slammed, followed by foot fall descending in the stairwell. A couple of men's voices spoke to one another in anxious tones. Their quarry had gone through a servant's exit and was escaping.

Two bio-mechanical men began their chase.

One remained. Why were the windows open?

He flexed his artificial right arm. His natural left hand made a fist. Slowly, he approached the blowing curtains, then suddenly tore them from their rods and pushed half his body out onto the sill.

A hatpin jammed entirely through the mechanism in his right shoulder from above, freezing the whole arm in place. Floundering, he turned to see two shoes – one small and one much larger – slamming into his body. The bio-man tried to use his one arm to grasp the ledge, but never had a chance. His enhanced weight worked against him and he dropped like a marble statue onto a wider ledge six floors below.

Mr. and Mrs. Sherman stood on the ledge, grasping anything that would keep them from following the now-unmoving body below. Mrs. Sherman quietly cursed the rigid bustle she wore and that kept her from pressing her back against the building. Her husband kept a surprisingly tight grip on her arm as they worked back to the open window.

Inside, he handed her part of the package and went to retrieve a carving knife from the tray of partially devoured bacon from the morning's meal.

She rushed over to the piano and took up her hat, then his hat and coat. "We need to get out. And when we're out, we need to look like everyone else."

He couldn't argue with that logic. The knife fit inside the breast pocket of his overcoat. Sherman carefully opened the door a fraction. No one was in the hallway.

He closed it lightly and nodded to his wife. Before he opened it again, he kissed her sweetly. Frankly, he was rather proud of her and her courage. She had the package and it was as safe with her as with anyone.

Turner and Forrer made it to the kitchen barely ahead of the two bio-men chasing them. The situation was a bit too familiar as they raced across the street and into the market, not daring to take the time to look back. If they could make it into the great park, then they had a better chance.

Something grabbed Forrer by the collar and jerked him backward. Turner stopped, spun around, and met one of the monsters with his fist. Turner Luck: he hit flesh not metal. The bio-man was moving so quickly that the blow flipped him off of his feet and onto the cobblestone paving.

Forrer put up a fuss by wriggling like a fish. His captor couldn't keep a good grip on him and suddenly, Forrer escaped by sliding out of his jacket.

The creature let go of the coat and grabbed ahold of the package. Forrer refused to let go. It pulled him but he resisted until he allowed it to exert all the force it had to drag him close. Forrer leapt up and slammed feet first into the monster, who landed some feet further back. The package was in Forrer's possession. Snatching up his coat to cover and protect the package from being easily grabbed, he nodded to Turner and fled north.

Turner gave his attacker a harsh kick, slid his coat off his shoulders mimicking Forrer, allowed the creature to see a potential bundle, and fled south.

The Seller's Market was laid out on the cobblestone square in a perfect series of lanes and crossroads: a masterful grid filled with curiosity seekers and vendors.

Turner ran at full speed, earning glaring disapproval from the fine shoppers who were appalled that a man would act as such. They may have thought him a thief, considering the way he was carrying his coat. Turner didn't care. He began working his way west, then north.

To throw his pursuer off, he shook out his coat, showing that he had nothing of value. The bio-man stopped, confused, then began looking about. People were staring at him and his enhancements. One woman screamed. His orders were clear – keep hidden as much as possible. The creature stopped, probably realizing it had followed the wrong man.

He quickly ran toward the entrance to the Market and down through an alley.

After checking to see if he'd been followed, Turner allowed himself a moment of breath, then started back into the Market.

He could see Forrer was just ahead of him. This was going to work.

But he last bio-man was not so easily fooled. He stepped in front of Turner, knocking him to the ground. Turner rolled, scrambled to his feet, and ran with the Devil behind him. Foolishly looking over his shoulder, he could see this bio-man had taken a couple of minutes to realize Turner no longer had the package. The creature stopped following him and began looking around.

The Market was packed with people he had to maneuver through, sometimes bumping them rudely. A blur of blue and white passed in front of him and he had one of the packages again. It was Forrer.

The remaining creature was hunting for Forrer now.

Near the end of the row, Turner took up a position to see if anything was following him, and to catch his breath.

Nothing.

There! He spotted Forrer, who had the bio-man close behind him.

The Lieutenant accidentally bashed into a woman beside one of the booths.

Well done!

The second package had been handed off to Forrer.

Mrs. Sherman reacted with appropriate alarm when the bio-man pushed past her, trying to catch Forrer.

Drawing up with a scowl on his face, looking every bit like the portrait taken just after he'd marched through the South and personally changed the direction of the War, Sherman shouted something about the bio-man being a thief who had just tried to accost his wife. People in the Market reacted to the commanding voice and presence. Several merchants and shoppers pounced on the creature and slammed it into the ground.

The bio-man was strong enough to fight off the men, including Sherman, who despite age, was not going to let other men defend his wife. The creature looked around wildly, unable to see Forrer. It resisted further attempts to stop it and fled out of the Market.

Turner drew in a huge breath, put his coat back on to the astonished gaze of several shoppers, and then headed out of the market with his package. By the time he was into the great park, he had buttoned everything up and was looking every bit the officer he was.

By the feel of the package, he had the top portion of the Relic with its scroll. That meant Forrer had the lower half – the Key.

Forrer would know what to do. That section had notes Turner had written for whomever would receive it – but he knew exactly where and to whom it was going. If this went badly, she would hate him forever. He had to trust her though – he had to believe in her.

Chapter 11

**TransAtlantic Pneumatic System (TIPSY) office
Eastport, Maine, United States of America**

There was every chance he was right; he'd been followed. It didn't matter anymore. After the package was weighed and the exorbitant price stated, it was sent on its way.

The TIPSY station was the terminus for the TransAtlantic Pneumatic System, designated as *Apostle Number Twelve* by those who worked on any of the thirteen stations on the system. This wasn't Forrer's first time seeing the mechanism in action, but it was the first time he'd been relieved of so much money for the mailing.

The Maine Station at Eastport was one of the eastern-most locations in the United States. It was also close to British Canada, and closest by far to Northern Europe. Hence, it was the final station on the system's line.

The operator was chatting casually with Forrer, not once noticing that Forrer's attention was on the huge tube stretched out behind him. Cast bronze, with a hatch opening to insert a delivery bullet, the left side attached to a room where the pressure generators worked so loudly that ear protection was required to simply open the door to the place. To the right, the Atlantic and twelve more stations between Maine and England. The floating stations had generators too. The pneumatic thrust was lost after a distance through the polished-to-perfection tubes, and thus each station re-shot the delivery bullets to the next.

He'd read that the first use of the TIPSY once it had opened was a handwritten letter of condolence from Queen Victoria to Mrs. Lincoln, whose noble husband had been assassinated. American folklore now, there was every chance the letter wasn't sent or some such difference in the telling. It didn't matter. The very idea was enough to get most Americans in a forgiving mood after learning just how much Great Britain had interfered in the Civil War, on the side of the Confederates.

The big tube, once laden by the package, had screeched its protest to such weight and yet fired the bullet on out into the depths of the ocean.

Sighing with relief, Forrer thanked the man for the local news, technical reasons his package almost didn't get sent due to the weight, and the small discount on the price.

He left the station office and walked down the long gravel road toward a small inn. He would have to stay put for a while. Returning immediately to the Old Men would signal that he had completed his mission and that it was possible look for the relic overseas. Every second counted; every delay was important, every gesture likely observed.

Whoever wanted the relic wanted Turner too. Well, now they were apart – mostly. One portion was away, and Turner knew what to do with the other. They needed to be apart: far, far apart.

Forrer pulled his cap down over his ears a bit more. In truth, he was a decoy regardless of Turner's plan.

Stopping halfway between the Station and the town, Forrer noted the appeal of the Maine landscape. It was attractive and quaint. And, for the moment, his location gave him a view of a man walking up the road toward him.

The man wasn't in a hurry but he was a tad oddly dressed for a typical Mainer or fisherman. He was overdressed.

"Monsieur Forrer?"

Forrer's hand slipped into his pocket and touched the pistol he kept handy.

The man held up his hand. "Please, no firearms. I have come here unarmed."

"Who are you and what do you want."

"Ah, straight to the point. Just like your commanding officer."

Forrer said nothing.

He could see the man more clearly now.

White hair, clipped beard and moustache. Fashionable suit, in the European Style. In fact, he rather knew the face, though he didn't know from where.

A little out of breath and genuinely using his cane to assist him, he stopped within a respectful distance, allowing Forrer to get a good look at him.

"I asked, who are you?"

"If I may introduce myself, I am a friend of Commander Turner's. I wish he were here to confirm this, but alas, his absence is crucial. My name is Jules Verne."

Forrer must have had the most idiotic look on his face.

"*Oui*. I know. Unbelievable, but I assure you and am willing to do what I must to prove to you that I am …"

Forrer held up a hand. "I've seen your photograph, sir. I believe you. But what are you doing in Maine."

"Making certain you succeeded. But more importantly, seeking to protect Mr. Turner if I can."

That made the hairs on Forrer's neck stand up. "Don't you work for …"

"I did. I have decided that my moral obligations to France should not preclude me from being both a good Earthling and a good friend."

"Earthling?"

"Are we not humans upon this Earth? Regardless, that is the one thing all men have in common. And I fear that things I have been made aware of represent a severe threat to France, to America, to human kind, and to my good friend Tom."

It took a full moment for Forrer to digest what he was hearing. Turner had mentioned Verne, but not with any detail, as though protecting the man. Why? He was just an author. But then, Turner had implied there was more to Verne than met the average eye. "Tell me more."

Verne looked around, satisfied that no one could hear them. "I believe that Monsieur Turner is in danger from unsuspected forces. My former employer, should he choose to fire me after this, is less of a threat than you may think. I understand there is an object of interest that you have sent away – no, please don't confirm or even tell me where, as I think it best you keep that your secret. However, if I could determine that this would be the best place to find either you or Monsieur Turner, those unforeseen forces may well conclude the same."

Forrer's hand touched the pistol again and he wondered if he would have to protect himself and this man standing in front of him.

"As I believe I am the only one here, I think Mr. Turner has succeeded in drawing attention away from you and your package."

"That was the intention."

Verne nodded. "I am glad. But now I fear that it will not take long for anyone to guess that Tom does not have the object and to take revenge on him for it."

"Why revenge? Why do they – whoever they are – want Turner? If it isn't your employer, then who is it?" *Let's hope no one knows Tom is hiding a portion of the Relic.*

For a long time, Verne stared at the ground. "I cannot say for certain but I will tell you my thoughts on this. I will tell you why I know what I know and every detail, as it is my wish to save Tom. I believe he is in more danger than any of you suspect. Perhaps more than I suspect."

"Details about your employer too?"

"Where appropriate."

"That will probably get you fired."

"It could get me killed. But for Tom, I will do this. Come," he gestured down the road. "We must leave right away. The sooner we find Tom, the sooner we can save him."

Forrer gave Verne a sharp nod. *Save him, from what?* He suddenly realized just how cold the air was.

Chapter 12

Residence of M.R. Gray
Sutton, Surry, Great Britain

"What is it? And what took you so long to get over here?" Miranda sat down on the couch next to Lettie and watched intently as her friend unwrapped the intriguing object.

"I had to send a telegram. I made a promise."

Layer after layer was removed, and it was taking so long that Miranda almost took it out of Lettie's hands in the hopes of doing a better job. But, there was no 'better job.' Whoever had shipped this to Professor Gantry had almost literally buried it in linen. And it smelled something awful.

"I don't know what it is. It came by TIPSY. That much isn't noted on the packaging, but I've been getting so many – things from all over –one can usually tell." She looked sad for a moment, then shoved her glasses firmly onto her nose.

"So," Miranda said, looking closer, "someone sent that five to ten days ago. That's a tremendous expense. That someone must, I daresay, want you to have it badly – if you can find it in all that wrapping."

Large strips of soiled cotton cloth fell away, one at a time.

"Miri, what is that smell? We should get those out of the house, quickly."

"Smells like someone wants to put others off – to keep them from opening the package."

"It almost works," Lettie said, kicking the cotton away. Underneath were other layers of cloth. Linen. These strips were of a much higher quality.

At that moment, Miranda took notice of the linen. It was old. In fact, she was sure it was ancient. The bandages were beautifully made, with an extremely tight weave – yet it was obvious it was not produced by a machine. There were variances in thread width, suggesting that perhaps the thread was handmade. Then, there were the faded markings. Egyptian hieroglyphs, she assured herself, confident in the knowledge that she had recently taken an interest in such things.

"I haven't reached the bottom of all this," Lettie replied with a modicum of frustration. "I stopped unwrapping it because it came with a note. Read it. Then I think you'll understand why I'm here with this thing."

Miranda picked up the small envelope on the table in front of them and slid out the handwritten note.

Ancient? Unknown purpose. Wanted by – (and here a word had been scratched out) *– dangerous man. Hide it far away. Very dangerous if known to be in your possession. Do not keep it close. Forget where you've hidden it. Be safe first of all. Tell no one.*

The rest of the note, written in another hand on the back of the card, left them both staring at each other and the wrapped object.

Found: 21 January 1876.
Discovered by: Emil Hertford, Professor.
Location: California, United States of America. Interior of Mt. Shasta Volcano. Ancient Temple.

The old bandages finally released their prisoner and Lettie barely caught it in time before it hit the floor.

"Impossible," Lettie hissed out of her lips.

"It's Egyptian." Miranda touched it.

"Impossible!" Lettie set it quickly onto the table, still partially covered, and let go of it as though it might sting her.

"Improbable. Unlikely. But here it is. Who sent it?"

For a long time, Lettie stared at the object before looking at the floor and whispering, "*He* did. I know his writing. I have that other note from him. That's why I brought it here, for you to see. I couldn't quite face opening it alone."

"Tell me you weren't worried it was an engagement ring?"

They sat for a longer time in silence – Miranda waiting for her friend to say what she had to say. The words seemed to be buried in the pile of linen wrapping.

Gathering her wits, Lettie took a deep breath. "Ancient and dangerous. This is very much your area of expertise. He wrote 'dangerous' twice. He wouldn't have sent this for – for romantic reasons. That's another reason why I came to you."

"Thank you."

"I have a bad feeling I've put you in danger."

"Thank you again. I was starting to get bored with all the bad manuscripts I've had to read. And as you know, I'm fascinated with archaeology, mysteries, and ..."

"Miranda – the note claims it's Egyptian."

"And so it appears," her voice showed her enthusiasm.

"Found in California?"

"Well ..."

Lettie changed her seat to better face Miranda. "Not San Francisco, in a museum. Not in some private collection in the state capital. Inside a volcano, if we are to believe this note. Which I don't. But *He* does."

Slowly, Miranda reached out to pull away the last of the relic's covering. "If this Professor Hertford found it inside a volcano, then it's your expertise here too, not just mine."

"Impossible."

"Improbable. Let's have a look at it."

It was without a doubt extremely lovely. Metal, which Miranda noted was not exactly a favored material amongst the ancient Egyptian statue makers, but certainly not unknown to them, if her teachers at New College were to be believed. Her mind sidetracked momentarily as she considered it unlikely that she would show this to any of them – at least not yet – since she was a tolerated sit-in student in their anthropology and archaeology classes. Well, Kit Moore didn't seem to mind her presence but some of the other professors were barely controlling their hostility. Money, however, had silenced them.

Back on target, she began to note the details. It was, in part, a statuette of a seated figure. No more than five inches long. A female. With a cat or lion's head and a damaged section on the head indicating that something additional had been located on top, but was now gone. Around its jaw and neck, and down its back, vines appeared to be wrapped around and often inserted into the skin.

The hands and feet were delicate and human. It was balanced on a short box of sorts, with one leg forward of the other – very typical of the art form.

The deviation from the normal statuary style was that a large wheel was protruding from the box, parallel to the figure, and that the lioness appeared to be turning it with one hand.

The wheel was a chariot wheel, like those one could observe in the temple decorations at Thebes and Luxor. From the center of the wheel protruded an irregular shape that made no sense whatsoever.

As both women examined it further, the wheel began to move. It was set by an axel into the statue but free to turn.

"Is that pumice?" Miranda pointed to some caked-on debris near the statue's base.

"It appears so, though I'd like to look at it under a microscope."

Miranda opened her mouth to speak when Lettie cut her off.

"No. If you have an Atlas available, I'll show you just how far California is from Egypt. And all the things in between that would preclude ancient travelers from making it so far around the world."

"Lettie dear, I know it's a long distance. But what if?"

Lettie sat back and stared at her friend. "If what? There is an ancient Egyptian temple built inside an American volcano? Really?"

Miranda smiled. "Look at this thing and tell me it isn't fascinating and compelling. Of course, the idea is ludicrous, but it is exciting."

"What can you tell me from your studies?"

"Nothing Dr. Moore couldn't …" She stopped, seeing the look of horror in Lettie's eyes. "He's still – unavailable, isn't he?"

"He can't be out in public. Not yet. Not until things calm down. The word got out about him. It's horrible what people are saying where before they were entirely complimentary."

Miranda nodded gravely. It wasn't fair. "He's a brilliant anthropologist and his work will outlive any – any accusations."

"I'm afraid there's nothing more we can do – for the moment."

Miranda took the object and began turning.

"You don't like something about it?" Lettie said, noting the scowl on Miranda's face. "You're the expert."

"I'm hardly an absolute expert. But – you're right. This looks almost perfect. I might not be able to detect all forgeries, but outright fakes I can. This is no fake. The shape, the detail, the proportions, even the bare breasts you know we modern British can't help but 'fix.'"

Lettie watched as her friend turned the statue upside down and squinted at the bottom. "So what is it that is bothering you?"

Miranda sat back and rested the object in her lap. "It's made from iron. Ancient Egyptians didn't work with iron until the Greco-Roman period."

"Assuming it is ancient – which I don't – but let's say it is – couldn't it be from that period."

Miranda shook her head. "I practically lived at the Museum when you were off in Iceland, and I feel rather confident in my knowledge of Ancient Egypt. Look here at this cartouche," she pointed to the oval hieroglyph on the left side of the statue's seat. "See those coils around the scarab? 12th to the 14th Dynasty. Middle Kingdom." She handed the object over to Lettie and fetched a large book from her book case. After a moment or two of flipping through pages of drawings and very small text, she stopped on a page with the exact same cartouche. "*Skheperenre*. 13th Dynasty."

"Apparently, your time was very well spent."

"We don't know as much as we would like to about this period. It seems Hyksos from the north were taking over Egypt and a great deal of art, literature, and architecture was lost to the fighting. All we have are some lists, such as the Turin King's list. And that list is fairly incomplete. Egyptians weren't entirely sure what happened during that period."

Lettie handed the object back to her friend. "Let's not get too excited. As I said, I doubt it is ancient at all. And you did note that iron is not a material generally used. And besides – look at it – not a speck of rust. It can't be that old."

Miranda was not so fully convinced. "Off hand, I'd say that this is Sekhmet, the lion goddess."

Lettie agreed. "So you feel that it is either an amazingly fine reproduction, with those odd alterations I daresay, or an original?"

"Improbable but possible. Let's ignore where the Professor says he got it. Why would ancient Egyptians add an articulated wheel to it? And what is that odd shape sticking out from the axel?"

"Almost looks like a key – the way the pieces are of differing …" Lettie stopped. "A beautifully made key. A key to what?"

"And we're still facing the biggest question; what are those tubes or vines or such that are all over her skin?"

Straightening her shoulders, Lettie narrowed her eyes. "I've seen that sort of thing before. On Hetzel's enhanced men."

"Those bio-mechanical monstrosities?"

"The very same."

"Which," Miranda stood up, "might explain Mr. Turner's involvement? Do you think he sent this to you to keep it out of Monsieur Hetzel's hands?"

"You know, Miri, there are times when I think I've gone mad and have spent too many hours reading those dreadful publications of yours. But after the last three years – the paranoia and extreme inventiveness are beginning to sound far too likely."

"Improbable, but never impossible. Do you think he sent this to you?"

"Yes. If for no other reason than he needs me to hide it."

"But if he thought of that, so might anyone who wants that thing. I think it best if it doesn't stay in one place."

"Yes. And I think he wants me to find out what this is all about."

Miranda tilted her head. "And are you?"

Lettie sat for a moment. It wasn't the first-time Turner had involved her in things she shouldn't have been, but then, the result was the most remarkable life. There was also the matter of her answer to his marriage proposal, which she decided was 'no,' of course, naturally – because there wasn't another answer, really, was there?

"Truth is, Miri, I like this sort of excitement. I love the hunt and the chase of a mystery or a puzzle. An ancient temple, with odd statues, hidden inside a volcano. Could this be any better tailored to me? There is a thrill to it and I miss it."

"Of course you do. When do we go?"

"'We' can't go – only I can." She reached out to take Miranda's hand when the dejected look flashed across her friend's face. "The only way I can think of getting to the United States is by stealth. I don't even know how I'm going to do that. Two of us will be even more obvious."

Miranda didn't even try to hide her disappointment, but such setbacks were not easily dismissed. "You're not getting rid of me. I agree, we cannot travel together. But I can join you once you're established in America." Before Lettie could try to dissuade her, she stood up and crossed the room. "I have an idea – several in fact." The dejected look was instantly replaced with one of cunning and cleverness.

Chapter 13

The Office of the Foreign Secretary
London, Great Britain

It came as no surprise to Lowell when he received the cryptic telegram from Professor Gantry. Well, he'd promised her his help. He would give it.

Several newspapers from New York, Washington DC, San Francisco, Edinburgh, Paris, and Brussels were laid out so that matching articles were positioned side by side. Two more American towns had been attacked by the mysterious speeding vehicle, leaving behind death and destruction. It was bad, according to the gratuitous details. Things were getting worse – the culprit was growing bolder – and the American Federal Police were no closer to figuring out what was happening.

One of those he'd been told to contact in America had sent a coded telegram to explain how it appeared that Hetzel had sent his unnatural thugs to try and take the package. Laying on top of all the newspapers was a notice from an informant in Paris, confirming that Hetzel was looking for the item and had now taken interest in the mysterious vehicle attacks in America.

Lowell had a horrible realization. The package and the attacks were related. He didn't know how but thirty years in the Foreign Office had honed his almost sixth sense about situations.

So. Someone needed to go to California and see what was happening around a spectacular volcano. Who else?

He didn't have all the pieces and now he'd need Gantry to do what his men couldn't. She was too perfect for the job. And deep down inside, he knew she would do whatever he asked, not because of coercion but because she cared. She liked the work of a government agent, with all its secrets and mysteries. And she performed quite admirably – for an untrained civilian.

The less he knew about the details, the better. How – he would leave to her. When – was now. What – he had connections to the railroad businesses there and one was trying to build a track right past the volcano. Perfect! He'd arrange for them to get the best geologist and volcanologist to do the feasibility analysis. Gantry of course. A part work, part escape from the madness of the world. Where – right in the middle of things.

Looking around and hearing the sounds of a functioning Foreign Office, he decided that his actions were in the best interest of Britain. He'd simply ask for forgiveness rather than permission.

Chapter 14

Lake Kirdall
State of Kansas, United States of America

Agent John Strock, of the Federal Police, held the letter and was never so glad secrets had been kept from the newspaper men. Strock was a great believer in the constitutional freedom of the Press and had seen that freedom work keenly for the sake of the American people. Keeping information from them was an anathema to his philosophy, but crucial in this case. The hypocrisy was deeply disturbing. But worse by far would be the result of allowing the newspapers to print the madman's letter. One need only look at the London riots to know how an insane man's thoughts in print could result in violence.

At first, he'd thought the mysterious attacks to have been nothing more than drunken stories. Then he'd seen it for himself in North Carolina. Now, there was no doubt in his mind. Strock pocketed the letter and quickly joined the fire brigade.

The story had changed, or so he was able to determine from the comments of his fellow bucket handlers. Pail after pail was handed to him, sloshing water out onto his trouser legs, as he passed it to the next citizen.

"Came out of the water," one man said. "Glowing lights out on the lake, then kaboom! It flew."

"It didn't fly until later," a woman corrected. "First it ran on the ground. After it came out of the water."

Strock tried not to drop the bucket handed to him. "Are you certain?"

The man and woman looked at each other. "No, not exactly," she finally confessed. "I saw it come out of the water. Sure as daylight. But then, it moved so fast."

The man had to add his observation too. "Faster than a locomotive. I could barely see it."

One thing Strock was convinced of, at this point, was that the mystery vehicle was both multipurpose and fast. But speed was relative to perception; in his father's day, a locomotive going twenty-five miles per hour was shocking and people were sure the human body could not stand the acceleration. Today, of course, locomotives travelled at sixty-five and seventy-five miles per hour without anyone's person vaporizing from the speed. Perception was everything.

Now, his concept of multipurpose was being challenged – increased, in fact. The thing could maneuver on the water. He didn't believe for one moment that it was partially a submarine boat. Or, could it be?

It took the citizens of the township a full hour of passing buckets before the building no longer had openly burning flames. No doubt it was still hot and could erupt back into flame again. That was when the Mayor and Head of the Cattleman's Association called him over. They'd found a body.

Well, it had been a body. A man? He was a bit short, but stocky enough. Burned to a crisp. Doubled up into a fetal position, clutching a box.

Slowly, Strock worked the box out of the charred remains. It had survived the explosion and fire. Before he walked away, he quietly prayed that the man hadn't really felt the fire – that he'd been dead before that point. Strock hated the idea of dying in a fire.

Inside the box was something astonishing – drawings of mechanical limb replacements. The fellow was trying to make artificial hands and feet for those who lost theirs. And not just wooden, static replacements, but articulated and potentially functional parts.

What was this mysterious vehicle trying to destroy? The attack sites had nothing in common, except brilliant men and laboratories. Now he had a whole new concept of the crimes.

As he went back to the hotel to write up his report – the smell of burnt wood and flesh giving him a piercing headache, Agent Strock read the letter one more time.

On Board the Terror

July 15.

To the Federal Police,

The vehicular invention you have witnessed will remain my own, and I shall use it as pleases me.

With it, I hold control of the entire technological world, and there lies no force within the reach of humanity which is able to resist me, under any circumstances whatsoever.

Let no one attempt to seize or stop me. It is, and will be, utterly impossible. Whatever injury anyone attempts against me, I will return a hundredfold.

Let both the Old and the New World realize this: They can accomplish nothing against me; I can accomplish anything against them.

I sign this letter:
Commander of the Master of the World

Why was it every crazed genius simply had to make grandiose statements, preferably to the Press? Was their supreme intelligence not enough that they had to seek the awe of the public? Strock wadded the letter into a messy ball and shoved it back into his pocket. The newsmen would no doubt report the incident, but if he had anything to say about it, the villain would not garner more than that!

Chapter 15

New York, New York
Broadway, Near the Battery

What Tom Turner felt prodding his lower back was neither a knife nor a pick-pocket's hand. He'd expected something, and if this was one of the attackers, he would need to stall as long as possible. If it was a common thief, then he'd have to deal with him.

He knew what it was, even through several layers of uniform: a broad barreled gun. Shotgun, double-barreled pistol – it didn't matter, though with the dense crowd he was standing in, a handgun of sorts made the most sense. The likelihood that there was a trigger and a bullet involved with the object made it impossible to ignore. "If you want money, you've come to the wrong man," Turner said dryly. "You must not know how poor a sailor's pay is."

A hand reached around his arm and pulled him slowly away from the crowd. The gun remained jammed into his back. Turner was forced to remain facing forward.

On the street in front of him, gigantic pieces of a metal sculpture were being carted down Broadway. There was no reason for the trip except to show off the brilliant work of the French artist and the generosity of the French government. "Dame *Liberté*" was already starting to oxidize in the New York air. Much of the statue was on the island in New York's harbor, but for the sake of publicity, and fund raising, several parts were being displayed to the crowds that packed the sidewalks. 200,000 people crowded the streets and docks. Everyone with a raft or yacht had found its way to the harbor. Were she a real woman, subjecting her sandaled feet, bare hands, and crowned head to wildly hollering crowds would be considered vulgar. This was as much a circus as Buffalo Bill's Wild West, who had himself paraded down the avenue only a week before.

The hand continued to pull on Turner, guiding him backwards carefully. Each time he moved back, someone stepped into the gap he left. Space was at a premium and all eyes were on the copper statue.

Roughly, Turner was pulled around to walk forward into a narrow alley between buildings. The individual with the gun remained behind him, unseen. The hand grasped the back of his collar and the gun was settled against the nape of his neck. Making any inquires at that point, Turner realized, would be a useless effort. His shoulders scrapped against the narrow walls, leaving a dark, Naval Blue catch of wool each time. At this rate, he thought, his sleeves would be worn away.

The narrow walk opened into a dirty, reeking, wide back alley, typical of New York's dockside. Laundry hung over poorly made steps and piled, empty boxes pretending to be stoops. Poverty was resourceful. Laborers lived here. Fishermen, stevedores, and longshoremen. Thanks to the arrival of the Statue of Liberty, no one was even here.

What was in reach? What could he use? A broken board. A drawer handle he could add to his fist. Something in a bucket that he could use to distract.

He was forced to stop. "I have a ten-cent piece in my pocket. That's all."

Someone laughed a little. An odd sounding laugh. Not loud or boisterous, but low, amused, and slightly mechanical. Perhaps the sound was even hollow?

Turner was thinking the possibility that he was being robbed was very slim now. This was an abduction of sorts. Commander Tom Turner knew all about abduction, having committed the crime often enough in the name of war – and sometimes peace.

"What?" he said sarcastically. "You don't want my ten cents? That's a meal's worth."

"Save it for your Bride." The statement came in a whisper. A slight metal, ringing sound followed as though the words were being echoed in a tin cup.

Turner stopped attempting to calculate his opponent's size and potential strength. Did the man say "bride?"

"She did tell you 'yes,' didn't she?"

"What are you talking about?"

"Don't play stupid." The tinny whisper shot back. "Your Doctor. Did she say 'yes' to the proposal you sent her? A TIPSY message – not at all romantic."

Turner thought he knew the voice, but the whisper and the metallic echo distorted it. "I don't think I want to answer that." He started to turn his head, to look at the man with the gun. He saw a shadowed face before being jerked by his collar and forced him to face front again.

"Are you ashamed that you asked her?"

"What? No."

"Then perhaps you're ashamed because you betrayed a friend to have her?"

Turner's heart began pounding. "I've lost many friends, but never over a woman. Who are you?"

The hand yanked him backwards and lips talked directly into Turner's ear. "I'm the one you betrayed. You were *my Tom*, my friend, my comrade in arms, before she came. You were my First Mate and you left me. I'm willing to forgive you. Come back."

Turner knew the voice. He dropped nearly to one knee and pivoted, his hand grasping the barrel of the gun and pulling it away. The man he faced never once tried to defend himself. The pistol slid out of his hands. He just stood there, chuckling a bit.

Taking the gun by the grip, Turner pointed it at the figure. It held its hands out in a mock surrender.

Turner's lips moved for a moment, searching for a sound. "Sir?" he whispered. Feeling was fleeing from his hands.

After signaling that he would not make a sudden move, the man reached up and pulled back a wool hood that had provided shadow for his face. Smiling out from underneath, looking more remarkable than Turner had ever remembered, the man laughed. "Shoot me, Tom. Or come back to me. Pick one and follow it through."

Then he laughed harder.

Chapter 16

Hudson Atlantic Railroad
New York to St. Louis Passenger Service

Verne was a consummate author; he looked for every opportunity to observe human behavior and to store away interesting tidbits for character development later. Mrs. Sherman was a treasure trove of fascinating habits and gestures, none of which any reader would believe existed unless they had the pleasure of meeting her.

He'd been told by Lieutenant Albert Forrer that she was elegant and fashionable. He would have to use his imagination for the time being; Mrs. Sherman was dressed in a Sergeant's uniform, sitting with one foot propped up on the opposite knee in a very masculine manner. Her hair was hidden under a very wide brimmed hat and her jaw behind a yellow scarf.

Naturally, the former General of the Army, W.T. Sherman, would be travelling with military men. Forrer was in uniform. It all made sense, even if Mrs. Sherman's ability to realistically mimic a man was a bit too good. Occasionally, when no one was looking she would give Verne a comforting smile.

At Harrisburg, they changed trains. The new car was first class and had distinct carriages that would allow them to speak more freely.

Mrs. Sherman held the carriage door for the gentlemen, all of whom outranked her Sergeant's stripes. Once inside, shades were drawn and doors locked. The lady took off the hat and allowed a single braid to fall down her back.

"I feel as if I must apologize, Madame," Verne said, holding his hat.

"Whatever for?"

"Am I not contributing to the need for this masquerade?"

She laughed lightly. "How very kind of you, but this is not the first time I've had to adopt a man's attire. And it would be necessary even if you were not here."

The poor Lieutenant, Verne thought, he kept trying too hard not to look. The idea of a lady in trousers must have been terribly uncomfortable to him; he should try his best to be open minded about such things. The train began jerking forward and he sat down long before he'd meant to.

General Sherman didn't appear to be happy about his wife's clothing, but not surprised either. To make up for it, he reached out to help her out of the uniform coat. "Gentlemen. My dear. I believe we're in relative safety and privacy now."

Mrs. Sherman sat, and rested her arms on her legs, leaning closer to Verne. "Monsieur. Would you kindly repeat to us what you told the Lieutenant?"

The author put down his hat slowly, taking extra time so that he could gather his thoughts. "As I have told you, I have been in the employ of Monsieur Hetzel for some years. He was and is my publisher, and to him I owe a debt of gratitude for my career as a novelist. I will not bore you with details. Suffice it to say that I do not consider my actions to be a betrayal of the gentleman, and I must insist that you think of him as one of France's greatest patriots. He has served Her uncompromisingly."

Sherman sat up, scowling. "By creating monsters?"

"Not all are. And yes, I too have my doubts about his methods but none about his reasons."

The General sat back, unsatisfied but willing to listen.

Verne shifted in his padded seat. "I fear that a prime example of what you fear has now been released back into the world. I should say, escaped. Unlike many of the other bio-mechanical men, this one has not – how shall I say this?"

"You're an author, Mr. Verne," Mrs. Sherman said in a flat, determined tone. "Surely words do not cause you consternation?"

"I don't wish to be blunt with a lady present …"

She glowered at him. "I can put the disguise back on if that will help. I assure you, I am not easily offended."

Her husband lost his scowl and set his hand on her shoulder. "If you promise not to make it into one of your biographies, we can tell you all about how this lady changed the War. But for now, I will only say that there are few stronger that I know of."

Verne was positively impressed that the lady had won such admiration. But then, of course, the General had married her after the death of his first wife; only a remarkable person could have penetrated the renowned grief he had possessed at the time. "This man, whom my employer tried to save, was not stable to begin with. He was experimenting with chemicals that were altering his mind prior to the attempts to use bio-mechanics to save his life."

"He's crazy," Forrer interpreted. "And he has a terrifying connection to us."

That made the Sherman's exchange glances. Forrer signaled Verne to get on with it.

"*Oui*, that is correct. Loose in the world, his insanity would be bad enough, but he will want to – to …" Verne almost couldn't say it. "He will want to add to his mad attacks on your villages a singular act of revenge that could have consequences on the group you call the Old Men."

"Spit it out, sir," Sherman demanded. "You're telling us that you know who is committing these murders around the country. A madman. An inventor of some sort of vehicle. And that …"

"Tom Turner. He will take his revenge on Tom Turner." Verne's eyes began to tear up.

Mrs. Sherman dug in her pocket and produced a handkerchief. She reached out and took the author's hand. "Focus, Monsieur."

Verne said something sweet in French, then spoke up. "He will want to hurt or convert Mr. Turner because he blames his situation on Tom. And if he converts Tom to a bio-mechanical being, he may also obtain information about the Old Men from him. I can say with absolute certainty that the most fearful thing to Mr. Turner would be to become one of those, as you say, monsters."

"Who is it?" she squeezed his hand, begging for a clear answer.

Chapter 17

New York, New York

Robur.

Robur the Conqueror

Turner lowered the gun, surprising himself, though apparently not Robur. It was not what he had been trained to do. When confronted with an "enemy," one outmaneuvered the enemy, disarmed them, and created a defensive position or advanced aggressively. Turner dropped his guard completely and against common sense at the sight of his old, commanding officer. Robur, creator of the *Albatross* and the *Indomitable* – flying machines – airships - stood in front of him, unafraid.

The man was dead. Captain Jean Robur had died.

"God, Tom, if you could see the expression on your face."

Turner said nothing but stepped closer to his former captain to look at what had happened to him. What he could see was hideous and beautiful.

For his own case, Turner knew his own throat had been disfigured and had healed badly. That was due to poor hospital facilities and equally poor medical treatment during the War. Dear God, how things had clearly changed. "Sir?"

What he looked at was a miracle of science.

Robur had been dead.

He should have been dead.

Robur stepped forward, knowing that Turner needed a better look. Where Turner's scar, a thick, dark strip that encircled most of his throat, was ugly, Robur's "treatment" was almost exquisite. Along the left side of his jaw, stretching up into the side of his cheek was a formed sheet of gold tinted metal. The jaw piece appeared to be sculpted to suggest a closely clipped beard, which matched Robur's real beard on the opposite side of his face. On the face-plate, the curve of a trim moustache arched down towards smooth, gold lips. His skin was forced beneath the edges of the plate and held in place by what looked like rivets. The golden jaw was not articulated and Robur was forced to smile and speak entirely out of the right side of his face. Such a limit didn't keep him from grinning.

Two narrow tubes ran from under his full head of hair near his earlobe, and disappeared over his shoulder and down the back of his collar.

He folded his arms across his chest, which remained broad and strong as ever. All but his head had remained the same for the man Turner had known before. "I have missed you Tom," Robur said with abundant levity.

It took a full minute of Turner starting and stopping several comments until he stuttered out, "I thought you were dead."

Robur's expression changed instantly to sad. "I know. I thought I was dead too. I thought you were going to help me die."

Turner closed his eyes, recalling the smell of the jungles, burnt wreckage, blood. Robur's and his men's blood. The crash of the *Albatross*. Robur's dying wish that Turner end his suffering. Such a small request.

But Turner was suffering too, from a brain fever, he was sure. He'd dreamt that Hetzel had been there, taken Robur away, and left Turner to be killed. His eyes opened and Robur was still standing there. "I don't remember."

"I asked you to kill me."

Turner shook his head. "I think I …"

"You didn't." There was a tinge of anger to the statement.

"Hetzel? He was really there?"

Instead of responding, Robur used his hands to indicate all the enhancements to his body and face. He didn't need to say anything.

"It was, I thought, a fevered dream. That none of it happened."

"But it did."

"Sir, where have you been all this time?"

Robur brightened a bit. "Above Paris for many months. Then the South here in America. I found a place to build. My genius is flourishing again."

It took another moment before the mental puzzle was beginning to come together, piece by piece. "North Carolina?"

"Ha! You have been watching me, though maybe you didn't know it was me."

Turner stared at the ground while his head was whirling with images. Looking up, he said, "Only you could build a vessel that moves so fast. It's the *Indomitable*, with improvements. How? Did you lighten it, maintain the hydrogen power, how?"

"That's my Tom. I will tell you everything on the way." He turned to walk back down the alley.

Turner didn't move. In fact, he felt the weight of the gun as he lifted it. "I'm not going anywhere with you, sir. This has to stop."

Robur stopped, keeping his back to Turner.

Behind him, a footstep splashed through a puddle.

He spun around to find three men – all enhanced – two quite neatly and one very crudely. The crude man seized the gun in Turner's hand and crushed the metal. God in Heaven, the strength. The other two men grabbed his arms and twisted him around to face their commander.

"Time to stop playing soldier for those tired, boring generals. You have much more to do. We do. Together. You and I, as before. We will put an end to mankind's tinkering with nature. We will stop the madness of men."

"Sir. You've killed a dozen scientists at least. That is the very definition of madness."

What turned on him, in rage, was truly terrifying. Robur the Monster balled up his fists. "Self-defense! Do you think they want to leave me free? Do you think they believe that I am their greatest achievement? Every man who invents something new puts the world in danger. Only I can master technology. Only I can protect the world."

"Protect it from what?"

Wide eyes glared at him and then softened into grief. "From me."

Chapter 18

Residence of Professor L. Gantry
Sutton, Surrey, Great Britain

Nothing had made her happier than receiving the letter from Professor Pierre Aronnax. The gilded calligraphy of the Paris National Museum letterhead gave her an immediate rush of hope. To be wanted – desired: was there anything anyone truly wanted more?

She was not expected to teach over the summer months at New College. That season was nearly always expected to be filled with field work – something she had every intention of doing, wherever she ended up. Thanks to Aronnax, though, she had an exceptional offer to escape the horrors of post-Shaker England. And all its mad hostility.

She feared for Rajiv Pierce. Yet she needn't – he was safe with his uncle, Nemo. There were others in danger from the violence stirred up by the Earthshaker. Some could hide what made them different from the mobs, others could not.

She was lucky, and she knew it. Her skin – her gentility – her apparent status – all these allowed her to escape most of the vitriol and riot. Her position in life gave her chances to run away where others could not.

And yet, she had to decline Aronnax's offer. There were battles for humanity that most people knew nothing about. It was simply what had to be. She was no supporter of keeping secrets from the public in general, but some things – like Hetzel's monsters – simply required too much knowledge to understand. It wasn't fair. But it was true. She barely understood the details and she had lived through experiences with his enhanced creatures. This was too important not to pursue.

She had her own challenges. Small, by comparison, but damnable all the same.

Since she had returned from Iceland, in the status of a famous patriot, the Dean had been scrutinizing her every move. When would she be getting married to that fellow who had been involved with the Earthshaker business? Or to Rajiv Pierce, whom he felt was unsuitable as a foreign-born man but somehow just what she deserved. His implication that she was somehow romantically bound to Tom Turner, American and man busy elsewhere, had made her face flush. His comments about Pierce's Indian heritage had become so commonplace that she hardly bothered to react anymore. No, it was the Turner business that stuck under her skin.

How dare he assume, she had wished to say. But she didn't. That's not how decent ladies behaved. Instead she kept her demeanor calm and polite, and suggested that there were no such connections. If he was concerned, she had added, about the reputation of the College, she could ask a reliable source at the Foreign Office to have a quiet discussion with him.

The Dean had nearly exploded. How would that look, he demanded, if the Foreign Office became embroiled with the good name of the College!

Well, she remembered saying meekly, she could also resign her position if that was his requirement. But that too would become very public and she would not be able to sustain a lie on the subject.

Ah, the satisfaction. Instead of becoming angrier, his jaw went slack. It had been obvious that the Dean knew how that would look. Lettie, now a bit of a heroine after her escapades in Iceland and the good relations she generated between that country and Great Britain, could not be seen to be *forced* out of her job. They would blame the Dean and he would have to explain himself, frequently, to school donors as to what he'd done to push her out.

Satisfaction? No, not at all. Really, it was all very maddening. She worked hard for the College. She was an excellent lecturer and brought hands-on knowledge of geology to the curriculum. Her experience with the eruption of Krakatoa, her years of working on various volcanoes around the world, her potential prediction model – all of it contributed to the excellence she provided.

It wasn't enough.

It was never enough.

The politics of being such a famous woman were extreme and tiresome. The tedium of arguing every point before she could teach it – regardless of her knowledge. The religious intrusions into her science, her classes, her life! She couldn't eat dinner at a restaurant without someone demanding to know why she ate alone – a woman should never dine alone. If she wore the wrong neckline, it was commented on. Why hadn't she taken a stand about women's suffrage? When was she getting married?

Lettie stopped packing her valise and leaned against the lectern. She would miss the place over the next few months. She had some very fine students who would eventually make outstanding scientists. Well, she'd see the lecture hall again, soon enough. For now, the broken window near the door was too much of reminder of that evening and the consequences heaped on her friend. Politics and hatred – she wouldn't miss that at all.

Yes, *when was she getting married* – it was a nonsense question. She was past youth, past child-bearing years, past – past so much. If she believed everything society told her – and she did tend to believe it out of forced habit – she was just pain too old.

When was she getting married?

Never.

The Moores's carriage had waited for her. Such a luxury. But then, they were kind. And they felt somewhat obligated as she had come to see Kit in his time of distress, taking the train on her own.

Gathering her skirts and pushing her valise in ahead of her, she quickly climbed in and pulled the door closed. It was going to be a cold but quiet ride across the river to home.

The door opened again. A gloved hand was followed by an older man who arrogantly helped himself to the seat across from her. The driver was as surprised as she, and began to protest. The older man waved him off and looked at Lettie, as if to either implore or order her to do the same.

"It will be alright, for a moment or two. Please drive on. Thank you."

The older man nodded and settled himself back against the cushions.

"What do you want?" She wasn't being rude, simply to the point.

"Robur."

"Robur is dead."

The older man sighed. "The trouble with keeping secrets is that often, the secret has been too well kept."

"What's the point of having a secret if it isn't to be kept?"

"Depends on the secret." He looked at her, trying to gauge her disposition. He would no doubt discern her angry mood if he was half as good at his job as he claimed.

"What secret?" she asked.

"He is alive."

Why didn't she feel surprise? Concern, yes, but not surprise.

"Mademoiselle. He is, as we say, gone rogue."

"Doctor, if you please, or Professor," she corrected sharply. "I also don't know what you mean by 'rogue.'"

Monsieur Hetzel sighed. "It is an expression we use in the intelligence community …"

She held up her hand. "I know what the term infers. What I want to know is: what exactly do *you* mean by it? Have you lost him? Is he mildly disagreeing with some idea of yours? Is he planning on destroying the better part of Europe?"

"*Oui.* You understand. But, I must tell you honestly that I do not know what exactly his intentions are, except that he will likely want to deal with Commander Turner. He spoke of him constantly. And, as my agents cannot locate Monsieur Turner, it would seem *Robur le Conquerent* has found him first."

Lettie closed her eyes. The memories of life as a prisoner aboard the *Albatross* flooded back as though they had never left. Mad Robur, who had taken to opiates to expand his genius and fallen prey to the addictions and paranoia. Robur who had rejected his interest in women so much that when he could no longer hide his longing, he turned on Lettie. Robur who betrayed his own loyal first mate, Tom Turner, and tried to kill him. The vitriol he'd heaped on her. The look of unbridled desire in his foggy eyes. As if nothing had happened between those days in the East Indies and now.

Her hands felt numb.

In the street, next to them, a sweeping vehicle hissed and squeaked its way past, blowing debris to the side of the avenue and scooping it up onto conveyor buckets. Such a thing would not last long in London, she thought, as if changing the subject in her own mind might make the whole conversation stop. Between the fog, the garbage, and the nature of the place, Lettie doubted that such a vehicle would survive two months. On the new Parisian avenues, were she to ever take up the employment offer from Aronnax, it would stand a fighting chance. "He was dead. Mr. Turner said as much. I believed him."

"This is not the Commander's fault. As far as he was concerned, Robur was quite dead. But I felt that the Captain had more …"

"You interfered."

"I saved a life."

"You made a monster, didn't you! How much of him is one of your …"

Hetzel's shocked and angry expression cut her off. The driver could hear them.

"What did you do to him," she hissed quietly.

"We merely rebuilt his skull."

Liar. She knew better. She also knew to let the matter go. If Hetzel was not telling her now, he had no intention of telling her ever. No amount of anger or pushing would accomplish the truth. "So now, you have a problem. Which has become Mr. Turner's problem. Which may or may not become my problem."

Hetzel shrugged.

"Where?"

"We think he is out over the Grand Banks, off Nova Scotia."

Lettie let that sink in. She was being far too "nice." She had been hiding behind a mask of scholarship and propriety for too long. She owed this man absolutely nothing – not even being "nice." No more! She leaned forward and whispered with a hiss, "So, he's built a new ship, possibly kidnapped an American, and may have world-impacting plans. Anything you'd care to add to that?"

"I understand you are angry …"

"You know nothing about my anger."

"I need your help."

"You have your own *assistants*. One of them was spying on my home the other day, wasn't he? What could you possibly wish me to help you with? And you can forget my assisting you in converting Mr. Turner to one of your - things."

Hetzel set his hands-on top of his cane. "I swear on my life, Mademoiselle that I do not desire Commander Turner to be enhanced. This is not my intention at all. I only wish to bring Captain Robur back – to where he can be monitored and cared for. This is all I desire."

Lie number two.

"I also wish to have you and Monsieur Turner reunited. Call it a Frenchman's fantasy."

Lie number three, she noted, silently.

"I will be blunt. Do you have a gift from Monsieur Turner?"

"A gift," she asked almost too innocently.

Hetzel sighed in exasperation. No doubt he was thinking: Women. English women. "Did he send you anything?"

"A proposal I cannot accept. That is all." *I can lie to you too.* "What was I supposed to receive?"

For a long time, Hetzel sat back in the seat, resting his hands on the cane, but drumming his fingers. He hadn't expected her to say she'd received nothing. He looked at her, as though she might betray the truth. Lettie stared back, running comments about her innocence through her head so that her expression would support that innocence. Did he believe her?

The cane split apart at the top and Lettie found herself stared down the length of a narrow, sharp sword.

"Tell me again, Mademoiselle. Did? Commander Turner send you a package" He glared at her.

The blade was sharp, no doubt. But damn it, so was her wit. "No, sir, he did not." She flicked her hand up and across the flat of the blade, temporarily knocking it aside. "Get that thing out of my way," she hissed. "How dare you come into my carriage and act like some ordinary low-life!" Go for a deep cut, she told herself. "You are no gentleman. I shouldn't have wasted my time thinking any Frenchman might be."

That hurt, or so his eyes said. Good. It was meant to do damage.

"I have no package and you can go to blazes. You couldn't care less about anyone or anything. If you want to turn the world into your mechanical slaves, you'll need to do so with without my aid."

Slowly, sadly, Hetzel put away the sword. "Perhaps you are correct. It was not the act of a gentleman to threaten you. Please understand that I am a Frenchman, as you noted. It is my every existence. I believe in the Republic. I will do everything I can to protect it." He locked the blade down. "I hope you will excuse me. What I seek could indeed cause the very world you say you fear: a world of mechanical slaves and slave masters. What I know could easily be used against the whole world – that is why I keep it secret. When I die, the secret of bio-mechanics will die with me."

Except for the doctors who created it, work on your army, and the men you've enhanced. She still smiled. He was trying to see if she would confess to a confidant more easily than to an assailant. Speak softly, let him think you've fallen for his act, she told herself. "I honestly cannot help you. The last I heard of Tom Turner was a proposal of marriage I cannot accept."

Did he believe her?

"Then, Mademoiselle Professor, will you still help me? You can see the importance of keeping this work secret?"

She didn't reply.

"I have a plan in mind. *Oui*. But first you must go home and stay there. It is likely that Commander Turner's package has not yet arrived. I thought it had been sent by TIPSY, but perhaps not. He is clever. Will you do this?"

"I had hoped to go back to Krakatoa, to do research."

Hetzel became almost enthusiastic. "And you should! First, wait for the package. If it does not arrive in two weeks, then I will take you to the Indies in my airship. It will save you weeks in travel, giving you the optimum time to spend in the field. Is that not agreeable?"

"I really want nothing to do with all of this. My plan is to leave for the Indies as soon as possible."

"You must not." It was a command. He then softened. "It is important that you are present to receive the package."

"You don't know that he has sent it."

"None the less, I insist you remain put. For your safety."

"Are you threatening me?" She leaned forward, her first thought was of her hatpin and how quickly she could reach it or the pistol in her valise.

"Mademoiselle …"

"Doctor or Professor!"

"You were lucky in Iceland. You bungled your way into a situation you barely knew anything about. You will not be so lucky again. You will leave this to those who are better suited to deal with international or extra-technical affairs. This is not a woman's place. You haven't the capacity to understand the complexities of international politics and policies. You have consistently resisted your natural place in the home and have been lucky to have survived. This time I insist you remain at home where you belong and I will see to it you do not leave until you can hand over to me the package from Monsieur Turner." As if trying to make up for his callous dismissal of her burgeoning worldliness not to mention her personal freedom, he sat back in satisfaction and spoke in a fatherly, patronizing tone. "It is a simple enough plan, even for you. You will reap benefits from it. Can you not see that?"

How many things can go wrong with your plan? Let me count. "I think your simple plan is dynamically flawed and guaranteed to disappoint us both. First, as I did not respond to Mr. Turner's proposal, I do not believe he will send anything to me for any reason at all. I have tacitly rejected him. And the time you waste waiting is time you could use to save him or to find your precious package. I daresay your behavior now and in the past, suggests heavily that you have neither an interest in my survival nor in Mr. Turner's. Go to America and do your own dirty work."

"Alas, we cannot. I do not have the same connections in America that I do in Europe. Also, Robur himself lies between here and the United States. He will know if I am coming. I will try other means, but the best course is that you give me the object." He nodded, not expecting her to respond.

"And when the so-called gift doesn't come to me?"

"I think it is the only thing to save Commander Turner and to keep Robur from threatening you, every day, of every year, of the rest of your life. And he will do so, without any compassion, make no mistake. Once this is all done, you will be free to live your pretense of being a scientist to your heart's content. And, once I have possession of the package, I can take his anger away from Commander Turner and keep you away from his notice."

Lie number? – oh, she'd lost count.

Chapter 19

Exactly where he feared he might end up

The whole vehicle vibrated. Turner knew what that meant. He couldn't decide if the engines sounded bigger than those of the *Albatross* or if it was his sensitive head that was imagining it. Drugged? Of course. It was a wonder that he hadn't suffered some sort of bodily damage for all the strange chemicals inflicted on him. What was it? Oh yes, simple chloroform. Two men, in an alley, held him. A third covered his mouth and nose with a rag soaked in the nasty stuff.

Robur. Yes, Robur had been there.

Where was he? First, best guess: on board a new *Albatross*. The way it moved, he could tell they were airborne. Heavy winds? No.

He lay on the floor of the dark room. To his surprise, unbound. That was unusual – gauging by his last few experiences.

Had he been dreaming? There had been violent motions of the ship, but that could have been a blurred memory of being brought on board. There was something else. Voices. Lights. Wings?

Turner rolled over and pushed himself up onto his knees. The room was pitch dark, which spared his eyes any pain but left him disoriented. He reached out to touch items in the room, to feel how large it was or wasn't.

Boxes, canvas, wood – no, bamboo. Paper. All the materials Robur had built the *Albatross* from. It must be a new version of the ship.

The door had the standard slip-lock that all the doors on the old ship had had. Locked. No surprise. Voices.

Voices coming closer.

The door flew open and Turner protected his eyes from the electric light in the corridor. The two men from the alley seized his arms and pulled him onto his feet. "Good morning to you too."

Each took him by the wrist and arm, and forced him down the corridor. They were very strong, which hardly surprised him. Turner decided not to fight. Through the hatchway at the end of the corridor was a storage and docking bay.

In the middle of the room waited a vessel seated directly above a pair of doors. Folded wings and tail. Enough room for three, maybe four, crewmen. A Gatling Gun – the damn thing had a Gatling Gun. Before he could observe more, he was forced through another hatchway. The ship had to be huge to contain the vessel. This was not the *Albatross* remade.

Along the way to what Turner assumed was the Bridge, they passed other crewmen. None of them was whole. Each had some sort of enhancement: some crude and some elegant. One or two spoke. Some did not. Occasionally one would look up at him, indifferently or angrily. It was then that Turner remembered he was wearing his naval uniform shirt and trousers. He was the enemy.

The Bridge was not wholly unfamiliar to him. A large wheel for the helm. Several controls to adjust speed. The vibration was due to the rotors located fore, aft, and above. Windows represented one half of the structure.

This Bridge had entries at the rear of the room, where Turner stood, and at both sides. Robur and three crewmen stood by the port side hatch, which was open. A man, wearing a leather apron and thick spectacles stood in the doorway, facing them.

The man was terrified. All that was behind him was the open air, which raced by as strong winds. The ship rocked slightly and the man grasped the hatch.

Because the roar of the wind and the engines combined, he couldn't hear what the man was saying. Pleading, no doubt.

Robur was unmoving. He held a long, thick instrument in his hands. He began shouting. An argument broke out. The terrified man tried to get back onto the Bridge.

Robur fired his instrument.

Lightning flashed and streaked out to the man, piercing his chest in three places, leaving seared, gaping holes.

The man staggered back, paused slightly midair, and fell away into the clouds.

Turner stared, his heart and head pounding.

This was murder.

Slowly, Robur turned around, handed off his electrical instrument, and left the crew to lock the hatch. The Captain's face was a monstrosity – a combination of the pleasant features carved into the metal implants and the raging flesh. He looked up to see Turner and those features suddenly changed to joy. "Tom, my Tom. Here you are." He waved at the two men to let Turner go.

Turner didn't reply.

"What, that? No, you needn't worry yourself over that," Robur easily dismissed the prior few minutes. "Come, take control of the helm. Let the old days come back to you."

Turner didn't move.

"Come now, Tom."

He felt his head beginning to shake. No. No, he wanted nothing to do with this. Had everyone lost their minds? Turner looked at the Bridge crew. All enhanced in varying degrees. His mind began to spin.

"Now!" Robur shouted.

The two crewmen behind him took up his arms again and forced him over to the great wheel, setting each of Turner's hands on the spoke handles.

"Take hold, Tom. You of all people will be able to feel the improvements I've made."

Again, Turner had no words. Though his hands rested on the bamboo handles, he couldn't bring himself to grasp them. He heard Robur sigh fiercely and immediately he found his wrists being lashed down to the wheel.

"That's better. You can tell right away that I have increased stability. It was necessary." Robur stood quite close behind Turner. "I have actually reduced the number of rotors per kilogram from my original design. The *Albatross* was good. The *Master of the World* is better."

Turner glared back over his shoulder. "*Master of the World?*"

"I thought it had a better ring to it than *Albatross Two*. A much more effective and representative name, don't you agree?"

He stared out over the rim of the helm, swallowing the first remark that came to his lips. "Is that what you want to be, now, sir?"

"God, no. The last thing I want is to be responsible for this miserable race of humans."

"What do you want?"

"To stop the madness of Hetzel. He's not the only one who is or wants to enhance men. To make them into unstoppable soldiers. The Prussians. The Austrians. The Ottomans. For all I know, the Chinese and the Japanese too. It must stop and I will be the one to end it all." Robur began to pace behind Turner. "Do you think I want the world to become like me? Like us," he added, sweeping his hand out toward the crew. "Look what they've done. Well, now, I'm going to stop them – all of them. You saw my attack vessel in the hold?"

"Reminded me of the *Indomitable*, the vessel you build in the Indies."

"A ridiculous name but it sufficed for the time. This one is more appropriately named the *Terror*, and it is far more advanced than the *Indomitable*. It is the perfect vessel of war – my war – and is a superb extension of the *Master of the World*."

Taking a moment to absorb what was being said, Turner licked his lips before speaking. "That man, a moment ago. He wasn't enhanced …"

"He was one of them! One of those working to make bio-mechanics possible to any tyrant who is willing to buy the secrets. They are all against humanity and must be stopped. No one must ever know what it has been like. No one must ever be forced to become …"

Turner's mind filled in the rest: to become a monster. For the first time in minutes, he looked at Robur. The Captain had always been quick to change moods, something Turner had learned to deal with as his First Mate. But now, whoever it was looking at him with Robur's eyes was no longer Robur. "What do you want from me? I'm not part of Hetzel's madness."

Robur stopped and put his hand on Turner's shoulder. "I want you to join me. This is the most noble quest of any. To free mankind from the tyranny of technological subjugation. To keep more of me from being made."

It was beyond perplexing. "Your cause is noble, sir, but your methods …"

"Are necessary!"

"Killing people who might, maybe, contribute to bio-medical technology, is missing the true target. It isn't noble. It's killing – it's murder."

His hair was grasped and his head pulled back. "They are the murderers. They are the destroyers of nature." Robur let go with such force he slammed Turner forward into the helm.

"Not all, sir, not all. Why not go after Hetzel or the Prussians directly?"

The pacing began again.

Why was he trying to reason with a madman? He only knew he had to try and reach the Robur who had once existed, long ago.

"I cannot reach them. Not even with my genius – they are too well protected. So, I rip the support away from them. I remove the inventors, engineers, and mathematicians who would blindly give them more power."

Lettie.

While volcanology was her specialty and her source of fame, she was also known as a remarkable mathematician. God above, he'd sent the relic to her and if she wasn't a target of Robur's for that reason alone, now he might attack her because of her intelligence.

As if knowing what Turner was thinking, Robur stepped up to his ear and whispered. "Even if she had agreed to marry you, I could not spare her. She must die. She is part of the conspiracy. She is an agent of Hetzel's now. And she stole you from me. You were my Tom – my Tom."

A crewman arrived, dressed in a leather cap and goggles, a full suit of canvas and leather, and a box. On his belt, he wore a pistol, a thick stick, and a knife. He had the look of a messenger.

"Did you find it?"

"No, Captain. A package was sent abroad on the TIPSY by Commander Turner's colleague. It was not large enough to be the relic."

"Abroad?"

"We aren't sure, but one of Hetzel's followers, the author Verne, was at the TIPSY station when it was sent."

Everyone waited.

Robur leaned toward Turner. "You sent it to Hetzel?"

"Yes," he lied. "It looked like something of his and I didn't want it in the States. He sent men to attack us – to attack me – all to get his hands on it. It was nothing. I gave it back to him."

"Those men were mine. They were sent to hunt the package. I did not know until later that your Turner Luck had placed it in your hands ..." The Captain backed up, shaking his head. "No. That's not the whole story, is it? You would never cooperate with Hetzel." He stood, staring at the floor. Suddenly he looked up and focused on his crewman. "How big was the TIPSY package?"

"Less than a foot, including wrapping."

"The whole relic would have been too heavy and too large to fit in a TIPSY bullet. No," he returned his gaze to Turner. "You sent only part of it." Robur's expression was suddenly one of delight. "You divided it into two parts. Sent one away, but I know you Tom. You kept half. Which half? The Key or the Scroll?"

So, it was more than just a statue.

Robur signaled for two of his men to come forward and take Turner back into custody. Once Turner was away from the wheel, Robur touched the handles. "Although I'm sure you truly want me dead, I know you won't do it. You could have here – you could have tried to crash the ship, but you didn't." Robur's human smile was frightening. "You didn't and I know that means you are still mine."

Turner was at a loss for what to say – things had become far more that surreal.

"Oh, Tom, my Tom." Robur gripped him by the shoulder. "You will need to tell me what portion you kept. Where is it?"

"I sent it to Hetzel ..."

"Liar! Don't ever lie to me! I can see right through your deceptions. Tell me what portion you have and where it is. Then we can be friends again. You and me."

"I don't have it."

"I guessed that much, Tom. You wouldn't carry it on your person. And if you wisely broke the thing up, you wouldn't keep the pieces together. No, no, you would want them far apart, even before sending one piece off."

Turner was faced to the back of the Bridge – leaving him feeling exposed to the vagaries the room – out of his sight. The two men holding their captive gripped him so strongly, Turner winced in pain.

Slowly, Robur walked over to his messenger. The crewman unhooked the stick from his belt and began to approach Turner. Robur stopped him and took the stick. It was black, longer than a foot, and had a handle made of wrapped leather. A cudgel. A nightstick that many policemen had. Robur held the weapon for a long while. Turner waited.

"Allow me, sir," the messenger said.

"No. No one touches Turner but me. He's my Tom. Aren't you, Mr. Turner?"

In front of him, he could see a beautiful volcano. They couldn't be more than forty miles away. Even in the summer heat, its upper slopes were covered with snow. With the exception of a smaller cone on one side, the mountain was a perfect conical shape. Oh, how Lettie would love such a place.

Turner remembered clearly the first and second blows to his lower back. After that, it truly became a welcomed blur. The less he held onto consciousness, the less likely he was to surrender his secret.

Robur stopped and began laughing. "How foolish of me. This will never accomplish what I want. I know a better way."

Chapter 20

The Private Airship *Voyages Extraordinaires*

Everything was starting to go wrong – very wrong. Hetzel sat at his desk, listening to the wind striking the balloon silk alternately with the engines engaging to keep the marvelous craft centrally floating over Paris. It helped when his stresses overwhelmed his rationality.

That was when he noticed that he'd crushed the lovely china cup into dust.

"Have you located our quarry or Monsieur Turner?"

Freunde's assistant, a man whose enhancement consisted only of his left hand, kept his head slightly lowered. "No, sir."

"Do we know if the package has even left the United States?"

"No, sir."

"And Verne. Do we have any idea where he's gone?"

"We think, perhaps, America."

"But you do not know."

"No, sir."

Hetzel's head was beginning to hurt. "Of course, I will guess that Mademoiselle Gantry has left the country to …"

The Assistant looked up with some pleasure. "Per your instructions, sir, we have prevented her from doing so. On two occasions, she attempted to send a servant to purchase tickets for the East Indies. Those were blocked. She travelled to Kent, to see that …" his nose curled up in disgust, "… disgraced Professor of Anthropology. We observed her, openly, and her return to Surrey. Just yesterday I observed her myself, walking to her woman friend's home. She may be unnatural in her occupation, but in all else she is a typical Englishwoman with little to do but visit neighbors and drink tea."

The report came as a relief. "Keep an eye on the woman, but she may have simply given up for the moment. In the meantime, find Verne. I have a dreadful notion that he has decided to interfere."

"Treason?"

"No. But it will be, despite his belief he is doing the right thing for France."

Freunde had taken an interest in the Englishwoman. She was not at all what he had expected. She was not rail thin, pale skinned, and lacking a chin, as most of the English were – in his estimation. She was surprisingly fashionable and polite.

As she strolled down the lane, headed to the home of her friend, he noted the subtle, tailored suit of clothes, the hat perched up on her black hair, the veil drawn over her face to protect it from the climate, and her matching gloves and parasol. She seemed a little nervous, as though she might know he was following her. But of course, Monsieur Hetzel had told her that she would not be allowed to travel for a time – surely even a woman could guess what means were available to keep her person contained.

At the Gray home, she spun the parasol around to block the afternoon sun. He could only see the top of her hat. She knocked solidly and was allowed inside. He humorously wondered at the ridiculous topics they would discuss and stopped long enough to light a cigarette. He would watch the front door and would keep his man watching the back. She couldn't sneak out past them. All she could do is sit with another woman, speaking about the men they needed in their lives, clothing, who was seen with whom, and other nonsense gossip.

Inside the house, the housekeeper, who often substituted for a lady's maid, stepped forward to help the lady out of her jacket. A simple pair of hat pins allowed the hat to be lifted off her head. The lady looked at it for a moment and commented that it was hardly her style.

The tailored jacket was pinned into place, rather expertly, but would not have fit properly otherwise, corsetry or no. The jacket was too large, though not by a great deal. But any fashionable person would have noticed had it not been altered with the dozen or so pins.

Miranda Gray looked up and allowed the jacket to be removed from her arms. While she removed her gloves and reticule, her housekeeper looked out the window. The dress was not quite suitable for her coloring but it was tasteful. Though the hat was not to her liking, the finely tailored, heliotrope wool tweed was delightfully up to date. She never quite understood how a woman who preferred to dig in the dirt could still have such superior taste or interest in fashion. Perhaps that was just one more thing she liked about Lettie Gantry. And why she was so completely willing to risk the masquerade.

"Is he still here?"

"Oh yes, Miss Gray. Smoking out front as if this is some club of his. Rude French."

"And there's another fellow out the back?"

"Willie spotted him earlier."

"Well, they are nothing if not consistent. They are very good at what they do."

"And so are we," the housekeeper said with pride, as though pleased beyond measure that she was part of some grand plan to protect Queen and Empire.

In Miranda's mind – that was precisely what they were doing.

Chapter 21

Mid-Atlantic Trade Wind Route
Airship *La France II – Dirigeable France société*

The Steward looked at the gentleman boarding the ship and decided the fellow would likely sleep much of the way across the ocean. Older men tended to do that. He looked down to note that the fellow in question was Professor Christopher Moore, of New College of London. He'd be just the sort to want a brandy or two, which of course was a purchased item and, if of a good quality, was over-paid with the understanding that the Steward might keep the difference.

He noted the Professor's thick, deeply gray moustache and beard, and slicked hair beneath a stylish, if well worn, Homberg. The coat, with its passé cut and yesterday's tweed, was bulky and seemingly hid the Professor from prying eyes. A pair of spectacles sat on the bridge of his nose and he held the latest newspaper in front of him with a pristine brown leather glove. The one ridiculous item the fellow was carrying was an over-stuffed valise, yet otherwise, the Professor was the typical Englishman on his way to America via the flowing trade winds.

Inside the 16-passenger gondola, one found that four of the passengers were in fact crew. Each was resplendent in a naval-influenced uniform, with a bright French flag embroidered into the left sleeve. The gold bullion emblem of *Airship France* held positions of honor on both the right arm and the right breast.

Professor Moore settled himself into the last row of paid passenger seating. Removing his overcoat, he revealed to anyone caring to look that his suit was equally unflattering to his figure and left one with an impression that he was hiding some girth. He immediately took advantage of the changing room and toilet. He then emerged prepared for the journey, having swapped his Homberg for a smoking cap and wrapped a knit scarf around his chin and neck, settled into his chair, covering himself in a fine blanket of wool.

Within the hour, all passengers were on board. All men. Some immediately felt a sense of comfort, as though now travelling in their gentlemen's club. The interior of the gondola was painted to appear as if decorated in plush velvet and wood. Of course, no such materials with their accompanying weight could be allowed on an airship. Instead, many of the common items were made of sturdy but lightweight bamboo, hollow interiors, and gauze painted to look to be of a higher quality. Some fellows lit up their cigars, unafraid of offending a female, and began with their tales of woe with the feminine race. A few gentlemen were French and it appeared that the remainder were either English or Scottish. The discussion was conducted in a distinctly Parisian dialogue, which Moore was quite content to ignore.

Moore simply opened a book, pulled the blanket up further, and made every indication that he was disinclined to join the conversation. Meals were delivered to him on bamboo trays and he tended to his business quite privately.

The same routine continued for the five days it took to fly from Nice to Baltimore.

The last one to disembark, Moore had hardly said a word the whole time, but had been quite generous to the staff. One steward conjectured that the man was ill and going to the American West to take waters and enjoy the extremely dry environment. Another steward suggested Moore was on this way to meet a lover, following her across the sea. Certainly, none of them asked Moore — that would have been unforgivably rude, if not entirely inappropriate for the serving staff.

The original steward simply wished Moore a safe journey to whatever destination he was heading. Moore nodded, shook hands, and toddled down the gondola steps to retrieve his luggage.

Despite the liberal use of the airship's toilet, the professor headed directly into the station's waiting room and made use of the proper facilities there. It was best to have any human "products" left on the ground, thus passengers were encouraged to leave some of their natural weight behind. It was a bit odd, the steward noted, that the professor hadn't made it off the ship before …

Well, it was no business of his. Just because the man had been generous did not mean he had the right to invade the fellow's privacy. The Steward began the process of organizing the cleaning of the gondola in preparation for the incoming set of passengers.

During his cigarette break, though, he noted that he never saw the professor leave the waiting room facility. Well, that worry could be dismissed as he had been distracted by the work on hand. Still, he felt a slight affinity for the man who had not only been generous but polite. Respectful, even. Not something he'd found common with the average English "gentleman."

The professor must have departed when he was looking away, as a round-ish woman, dressed in black, emerged from the facility. Her face was covered. There was some money, he thought, too bad she wasn't travelling with them but perhaps not: he never knew what to say to the grieving. Shrugging, he let the whole incident go, labeled as unimportant.

At the Baltimore Rail Station, the conductor assisted a woman up and into the second-class coach. She was quite infirm, dressed head to foot in black crepe, face covered in a veil, and likely not wearing a very heavily boned corset as her weight showed clearly in the shape of her gown.

She was going to be a problem, moving up and down the car. People would be uncomfortable with a widow, and by her clothing, a widow still in deep mourning travelling amongst them. Never mind the fact that she was considerably over-weight and people had firmly developed opinions on that particular subject, whether based on fact or not. He tended to expect large women to be helpless, lazy, or rude, though he would be hard pressed to think of more than one example of such behavior — everyone thought that, so it must be true.

A fat, aging widow. This was not going to be a pleasant ride. The conductor hadn't seen a manifest, but he was willing to bet there was a coffin in the freight car.

He allowed her to lean on his arm and tried to block her from incredulous stares. People could be cruel. How could they know why a widow was out in public? For that matter, what business was it of theirs in the first place.

She was very grateful and sweet to him, as he helped her settle into the small but padded seat. He'd see to it no one was seated next to her. A widow should be allowed privacy and quiet. Strange, she was so soft spoken, clear in what she wanted and needed, and ever so grateful for all his assistance. Now that he could see a bit of her face under the veil, he could see that she wasn't aging – she was aged. She had to be in her eighties. Well, that changed a few things in his mind.

Suddenly, he felt rather protective of her. Maybe because he remembered his mother after the passing of his father. Or, perhaps she looked like all those photographs one saw of the Queen of England. His widow was not quite as stout as Queen Victoria, and in a deeper state of mourning. Yet, there was something grandmotherly and kind about her. His heart went out to her.

Politely, he waited until he was back outside the coach before looking to see who she was. No one he recognized by name, and he had to admit he was relieved when it appeared she was only headed to Saint Louis. Not far. Two days at most, depending on any number of possible delays. He looked up to see the Airship France dirigible lift into the evening sky. Nope! He would much prefer keeping his feet firmly on the ground. One storm and he'd never be able to hold himself together. Better by far the steam engine and rail system.

On day one and one half, the conductor arrived fresh from his evening's slumber to assist the widow. They'd arrived at the St. Louis Union Pacific station with only a few hours of delay: two freight trains with priority passage, one very odd looking – new-fangled train that he esteemed had no business on his rail line, and a fallen tree across the tracks. Not too bad, as things went.

Stepping into the coach, nodding to the conductor going off duty, he quickly walked back to the widow's seat – to find it empty. Where had she gone?

"Mikey?" he called to his off-duty colleague.

"Yeah?"

"Where's our favorite passenger?"

"Mrs. Watson? Disembarked. Oh, hey, I forgot. Sorry about that. She left a note for you and for me. Got it right here."

Mikey handed over the envelope. Inside were several dollars crisply folded inside a charmingly written *thank you* note. For himself, he'd not been one to require or expect a gratuity. Especially not from second or third class passengers. But, this he felt was a sweet goodbye and thank you from one of the easiest passenger he'd ever handled.

Inside the station, the widow leaned heavily on a walking cane as she shuffled in the main door from the passenger platform. A porter approached her and she used the cane to point out which items of luggage were hers. Sensing his day was about to be unduly grim, he gently inquired after a potential coffin.

The widow shook her head and whispered that the important delivery had been made a week before hand. She kindly set a black gloved hand on his arm and thanked him for his kindness.

"Mrs. Watson?" the man asked, almost chuckling. He stopped when he was met with a disapproving glare from both the lady and the porter.

The fellow was dressed in an ill-fitting suit, with pockets full of gadgets. His tall hat had a card in the band and a pair of leather spectacles seated on the brim. White whiskers bounced as he spoke. "My deepest condolences, Madam. If this fine fellow will just bring your goods over here, we'll get on our way."

The porter appeared distrusting, but the widow patted him gently on the arm and told him this would be fine.

The fellow with the whiskers then offered her his arm and slowly walking her toward a platform much further away – one reserved for private rail.

"I hope your journey was pleasant?"

"I hope this is the last mode of transport for a while."

"It's the only one worth travelling on," he said with some flourish. "Designed it myself."

"Have you named it the Flockmocker Express?" she asked, glancing around to make certain she was not heard.

"And why not!" He steered her over toward a small waiting room, where the porter dropped everything else off. She insisted on tipping the porter, who then glared a little at Flockmocker before tipping his hat to the widow. The door was shut behind him.

"It's good to see you again," she said warmly.

The waiting room had windows but all made with frosted glass. It was private.

Lettie stood up and stretched. She'd been bent over for nearly an hour without relief.

Flockmocker opened the door a crack to look outside. "No one's around. The train's not here yet, but we'll know when it is. A redesign on my older model engine. Distinct sound when getting up to speed or slowing down." He looked back at her as she tried to straighten up. "Didn't that hurt?"

"Excruciatingly. But, I'm not sure how much choice I had."

"Well, you get another disguise."

Lettie stared at him. "Another? I think I've done rather well so far and I doubt anyone knows I'm here."

Shaking his head, Flockmocker closed the door. "We know. And if more than one person knows, then others know. It's a truth of the game we play, Madam. Always assume it."

"Speaking of those in the 'know,' I should like to thank Mrs. Sherman for connecting us."

"It was some bright thinking on your part, I must say. How did you know to contact her and how did you manage it?"

Lettie smiled, rather pleased with herself. "When I was in Kent. A friend of a friend sent the request to the one person he was certain no one was watching. I was a little surprised myself. Mr. Turner spoke often of General Sherman and I had done a bit of reading on him. It made sense when I was told. And it worked out grandly."

"Commander Turner would be proud. He has a flare for the dramatic."

She stopped pinning her hair back into place. "You still haven't found him?"

Flockmocker only shook his head. "We only know he was last seen in New York." He was genuinely grieved. He stared at her for a long time, his eyes expressing his mood. "I should have found him by now. We should have. At this point, no one knows if it's Hetzel or some new ..."

Lettie reached out toward him. "I don't believe Hetzel has him. Several pieces of information truly confirm this."

The white head seemed to nod, just a bit. "For now, I'll believe the evidence you say exists. But remember, I worked with the man for a few years – he is unpredictable."

"He sent those monsters after you." When Flockmocker looked surprised, she added, "My friend of a friend was informed, and fearing for my safety, gave me fair warning. Have there been any attacks on you or others working with you?"

"Not since Turner disappeared." He slammed his fist into his hand. "And the attacks on towns across the country are still happening. We don't know why but they seem to be targeting rather random targets."

"A moment please." She indicated that Flockmocker should at least turn around while she changed. How odd that this scenario would never have been acceptable to her only a year before. This was a perfect time to redirect Flockmocker's thoughts. "Tell me about the targets in these towns?"

"You don't need to worry about them. You have enough to worry about with finding the source of the device and any clues to the whereabouts of Turner. We'll be headed to California straight away."

"I'd still like to know." She unbuttoned the blouse and all the stuffing fell out. "Just to keep my brain turned to something useful. Humor me?"

With a sigh, Flockmocker shrugged. "Let's see. First there was a small town in North Carolina. Uh, that madam, is in the South."

"Yes."

"Ah, well. The quaint villagers say that the vehicle that attacked was incredibly fast – almost too fast to see. But it reportedly was at once in the air and on the ground."

The skirt, padded for the disguise, dropped to the floor. "Sounds like something you would make."

"Never for the air, Madam. I've lost my taste for air travel. Something about seeing the *Albatross*, Robur's ship, crash in flames to the ground."

"Didn't I see you shoot it out of the air?" She stopped to roll her eyes at the disguise she'd been provided. It wasn't going to work.

"Indeed!" He was perking up. "And if I can do so, so can another. No air travel for me. Now, about the targets. After North Carolina, the so-called vessel seemed to encamp on a peak in the mountains. Lights. Glowing things. Loud noises. You'll appreciate this. They claimed the mountain had been a dormant volcano come to life."

Lettie barked a laugh that was hardly ladylike. "Heard that tale before, and I daresay, I'll hear it again. In North Carolina? The American East Coast? Heavens – I do so wish they'd leave geologic conjecture to the scientists. I'm all for amateur experimentation and exploration, but one surely must apply the scientific method if it is to be of any value. There are no volcanoes on the American East Coast."

"Precisely. But by the time the Federal Police got there, our villain had moved along."

"Of course."

"Let's see. Oh, our man – and I hope you are not offended that I am presuming it's a man – has now added submarine capabilities to the vessel's roster. Came out of the water in Kansas. Quite the multipurpose vehicle – air, land, and sea."

Did Flockmocker know about Robur, Lettie wondered for a moment. She decided to wait before bringing up the Captain. "The American West offers more open spaces to test the vehicle. I would expect that there would be fewer human targets the further from the Eastern Seaboard one gets. Until one gets to San Francisco, of course. And no, I'm not offended." She began buttoning up the shirt, with the buttons on the right side, which made her think before accomplishing the deed. It was backwards to her experience. "What sort of people were being targeted. Never mind the location."

"Small towns with an average population."

"Scientists? Inventors?"

"Many of the targets had laboratories too. But not all of them."

"American aristocracy? Rich men? Powerful men?"

Flockmocker stopped for a moment to consider her suggestion. "Always some fellow with more than his neighbors. But not what I'd call powerful. More like, big spenders. Fellows who like to show off what they can buy but are too decent to keep it."

"Museums? Galleries? Theaters?"

"Two – private collections of ancient artifacts." He turned around before she was ready, but at least she was covered properly. "You may be touching on something there, madam. I've seen the object in question and it looks as though it should be in a museum. Or a laboratory."

"Or both," she confessed. "I have a terrible suspicion that your villain is after the Relic Mr. Turner found. He is or was looking for it amongst collectors. And, it would seem that he doesn't want it as much as he wants to destroy it."

Nodding, his white whiskers following his frown. "And you now possess the Relic." He folded his arms tightly. "Frankly I was glad to be rid of it. Looks like it came back home to roost. And I must say I don't like that your luggage went into baggage cars where it couldn't be guarded."

"The Relic is safe," she countered.

"Nonsense. Your luggage could be searched while you're nowhere near it."

"I imagine it was, Professor. I imagine you will search it too. You must. It's imperative that you do so, if only to do your job correctly. I'd expect nothing less."

He gave her a questioning eye. "We're not going to find it, are we?"

She didn't reply.

"Well, Madam, once we get to San Francisco, you'll go north to the Cascades. We're going south to Mexico in case this is the work of the New Confederacy. We must find Turner. We need to know what, or who, is behind all this."

She walked over to the gentleman. "We will."

"You of all people must get Turner back home, safe and sound."

At first, Lettie was surprised. "I will do everything …"

Flockmocker looked at her as though she were a specimen. "You, Madam, of all people. That is why you are here. To get him back."

All she could do was open her mouth.

"Don't think I didn't notice how he looked at you, when we were in the Indies. I've read about what you two have been up to, either together or apart." He wasn't surprised when she couldn't reply. "I may be old and daffy, but I know love when I see it."

Chapter 22

North Pacific Basin

The *Master of the World* was an elegant vessel. Like its predecessor, the *Albatross*, it was a flying Clipper Ship made with the most minimal construction possible. Bamboo, wooden nails, lacquered paper for walls – light and strong. Nothing ornamental or unnecessary was allowed. Which was why Turner was surprised.

The ship cut through the cold water, dipping bow down into a swell, only to pop back up on the other side. For those few seconds, Turner was under water, with stinging salt flowing up his nose and raking his skin. Fate alone allowed his hands to be reasonably protected. Or the Turner Luck.

Where any elegant ship had on its bowsprit an emblem of the name or the owner, in the form of a ship's figure, the *Master of the World* had none – until that afternoon.

Turner gasped and drew in as much breath as he could before the bow pierced the next ocean swell. There were mere seconds between slamming waves that struck him with enormous force. He was soaked to the bone, water draining down his legs.

He was the figurehead on the ship, where there had not been one before. Lashed tightly to the bow, his hands were up behind him, protected by his body. Why he was worried about his fingers in such conditions was a guess to him, but he was grateful that though they were wet, his hands were protected. Perhaps it was a simple fear of frostbite, which was possible. It was something a sailor or soldier had to protect himself from. He could lose toes or ears, but not the finger that pulled the trigger.

The *Master* began vibrating. Forward momentum was slowing. The rotors were spinning. A moment later, the vessel was ten feet above the highest swells. A moment later, Turner could hear Robur calling down to him with the same question he'd been asking, over and over: *Where did you hide your half of the Relic?*

Why, he didn't know, but Turner burst out laughing. He hadn't enough breath for it, but he couldn't stop laughing. What a sight he made. Instead of a buxom woman in some sort of flimsy dress, the ship had a half drowned, middle-aged sailor of questionable honor. It wasn't quite like keel-hauling, but the results would be the same. He laughed as though that was the only reply he had left in him. He laughed like he'd lost his mind. He laughed until he couldn't anymore.

Robur made some disgusting sound and the ship then began to rise.

Turner gasped for fresh air and remembered some of the facts an airship sailor needed to know. The higher the craft went, the colder the air. If the torture wasn't to be nearly drowned every time they hit a swell – water rushing into his mouth and nose – then he now faced being frozen.

As they began to rise above the clouds and the cold wind tore at his flesh, he could hear some of the men climbing down toward him. Robur wouldn't kill him today. Perhaps not even tomorrow.

In the distance he could see the snow-capped volcano. The ship began her turn toward it.

Turner closed his eyes and thought of the night, in the hot and humid Indies, when they had almost – almost made love. He'd touched Lettie. He'd felt her breast under his fingertips. She'd let him. Frozen air or frozen water – he would hold out. For her. For the woman he knew he would marry someday – madmen and Robur the Conqueror be damned.

He felt hands lifting him away from the bowsprit. What did Robur plan to do with him next?

Chapter 23

Union Pacific Station
St. Louis, Missouri, United States of America

Lettie stared at the "railcar," then at Flockmocker, then at the railcar, then back to Flockmocker.

"It runs," Flockmocker said, not looking up at her.

With a deep sigh, Lettie pulled the duck-billed cap down further over her forehead. This was not going in any way toward promising. The tweed of her costume was scratching at her legs, making her wonder almost aloud at how men and boys could put up with such discomfort in the name of fashion. It had been her experience that a corset, having worn one all her life, was actually quite accommodating and rarely demanded a scratch. Jodhpurs? Such a name for the ridiculous garment. Jodhpur was a kingdom in India and apparently, the Maharaja's son thought it was time to spice up English riding attire. Though it more than suggested the shape of her leg from the knee to the ankle, there was a plethora of fabric concealing all else above the knee. This was likely the only reason she finally relented and a put on the young man's attire. Knee downward, her leg was wrapped in a bandage-like covering over a stocking, with some stuffing to make her calf look masculine. Working shoes. A bloused jacket. Hair hidden.

If the costume fooled anyone, it was a miracle, but better than nothing.

"Professor," she said at last. "You do understand that out trip West is supposed to be incognito?"

"Of course. My friend and fellow engineer here has planned it to the nth degree. Post-war, he was an expert at this sort of thing."

With that glowing report, Lettie turned to glare at the man checking the front of Flockmocker's railcar. She guessed that the gentleman was about Flockmocker's age, sturdy and healthy, white haired, and cursing the mechanized contraption with a long string of Shakespearean insults.

"AG," Flockmocker shouted, as if the man couldn't hear well, "We leave in five." As if intending to start an argument, he held out his five fingers and began ticking them off one at a time.

AG grinned with enormous strain, nodded at her attire, and went back to insulting the railcar.

"Trust him, Dr. Gantry, he's been doing this for a long time."

"I look like an idiot."

"You look splendid."

"I look like a woman trying to not look like a woman."

"Sometimes absurdity is marvelously invisible," AG said before Flockmocker could reply. He stood up, cleaned his hands with a rag, and strolled up to Lettie. He had a good face, bright eyes, and plenty of experiences furrowed into the lines across his forehead. "As far as we can learn, your French friend is quite convinced that you have remained in England." His voice suggested a certain sarcasm.

"I'm very lucky to have a brave set of friends. I was assured that Miss Gray and the real Professor Moore will be protected – though I must say I'm not pleased to learn there may be American agents in my country." When AG smiled at her comment, she added, "Just as I'm sure you are not pleased that there are British agents here in the States. It is the game, is it not?"

"Agreed. Arrangements have been made for you to work in California, but with the caveat that you do not wish any publicity whatsoever. The railroad is vitally interested in getting clearance to build their line through to Klamath Falls and further to Seattle – your eventual report is desperately needed. They'll bank on your reputation once you've headed home. All very legitimate and relatively logical."

"That takes care of the foolish, the unenlightened, and the average conspiracy theorist. However …"

AG held up a hand. "There remains those who take an unhealthy interest in your whereabouts, who generally tend to be intelligent enough not to fall for the old 'dress her like a boy' routine. They will assume you are just another decoy, and will continue looking elsewhere."

Lettie shook her head, looked at the railcar, and back to AG.

"It runs," he replied to her unspoken disbelief.

Before she could muster her disappointment and embarrassment into a timely rebuke, she decided to ask about the transportation. "It is a bit obvious, don't you think?"

AG, Flockmocker, and Lettie all stood there, looking at the damn thing.

"I've run this from St. Louie to Frisco and back," Flockmocker declared, planting his thumbs in his suspenders and looking the stereotype of the mad, hands-on inventor. Jules Verne couldn't have invented him. "Anyone looking for you or spying on us won't really see any irregularities – we are quite irregular to begin with."

"Professor, Mr. G, someone's life is at stake. Quite possibly hundreds of lives. I don't believe …"

"Doctor," AG jumped in. "The world has become increasingly absurd. You're chasing a mad man in a fantastical vehicle who is supposed to be dead …"

"Ah, so you do know about Robur."

"Indeed."

Flockmocker, however, did not. "Wait just a minute!"

AG held up his hand and Lettie spoke up, "I'll explain everything once we're underway. If I may use an American euphemism, I believe we should lay our cards out on the table for everyone to see."

The inventor turned to AG with a cross expression. "All our cards!"

The engineer was unperturbed. "As I was saying about absurdity, we race back and forth across a continent in four days that twenty years ago could only be crossed on foot or horseback in two weeks. We receive our mail and international shipments by air. We can send messages either by wire or in physical form within a day to Europe. You, yourself, dealt with a man who could cause earthquakes. Absurd is our normal state of being."

"If you want something plainly normal," Flockmocker chimed in, "we could always get AG's old partner – he was about as straight laced …"

"Leave him out of this. He's retired to the Solomon Islands."

With that, Flockmocker threw his arms in the air, snarled something, and suggested that they board up.

Lettie took one more look at the vehicle, perhaps with a kinder eye. It was long, perhaps seventy feet or so. The nose came to a sharp wedge at the front, likely as a wind splitter. It had a cow catcher off the front, designed to complement the aerodynamic front end. The engineer's door and seat were surprisingly far forward, suggesting that the boiler and firebox were not of the usual design. Not surprising. Passenger or cargo boarding was from a central door, flanked on either side by large, round, porthole style windows.

It was painted in livery green with gold striping. At the front, it bore the designation, "3 and ½."

"What happened to the door?" It appeared to be the original door, with huge repairs and hammered out dents.

AG and Flockmocker exchanged glances that seemed to ask, *are you going to tell her?*

The interior, she found as she climbed up the four folding steps, was charmingly spare but comfortable. The windows provided a remarkable amount of interior light in the rear portion of the car. A couch split the back portion in half, allowing for two desks, a table with secured scientific equipment, and a pair of overstuffed chairs.

"Professors, make yourselves comfortable." AG saluted and headed forward.

The area between the front passenger section and the engine was closed off to accommodate two boat-sized sleeping rooms and a lavatory. A windowed, sliding door made the final separation to the engine.

In a moment, the usual sounds of a steam engine echoed around them – items of delicate material rang after bumping one another – and the vehicle started forward.

An all-in-one train, she thought, and suggested such a designation to Flockmocker, who spent the next hour, as they headed West, trying to work together her suggestion and his own last name – both being required in his estimation.

Chapter 24

Sutton, Surrey, Great Britain

The manuscript was not unusual – it was the standard horrible story filled with terrors and gore – the very thing that sold plenty of copies of her gazette. Miranda tossed the pages down onto the floor at her feet and decided to call for a fire to be made up. The room was getting colder quickly since the sun had set. Even with the curtains drawn, which they needed to be to protect what was going on inside the home from outside prying eyes.

The front door slammed and before she could do more than stand up, a man forced open the door and looked around the room wildly. He began to swear in French.

Miranda put her hands on her hips and glared at him.

Ignoring her, the man began walking around the room, still cursing.

He only stopped when Miranda replied, in excellent Parisian French, the same vitriol he had been spouting. She added flourishes that in English would have gotten her banned from gentle society.

That got his attention.

"Where is Mademoiselle Gantry?"

"Doctor Gantry, you mean? Professor is the other acceptable term."

"Where is she? She came in here – today – she …" He stopped and looked at her clothing. It was the suit he'd seen his quarry wearing earlier. Or had he?

"She's not here as you can see, so you can feel entirely welcome to leave my house immediately."

"Where did she go? Why are you wearing her clothing?"

Miranda stuffed her hands in her pockets, smiled sweetly, and replied, "I think her taste in clothing is rather splendid, though sometimes I do wish she'd add more silk to her daily toilet. Still, it is appropriate for a Professor. Very tailored …"

"This is not happening," he mumbled in French. Realizing that Miranda could understand him; he drew a knife from a sheath on his belt.

"And this is where you, being the big, strong, scary Frenchman, threaten me with your little knife."

He looked at the wide blade. "Not so little."

"Positively miniscule in comparison." She pulled a snub-nosed, Bisley-grip .45 from her pocket and pointed it at him. "What a world we live in where everyone is armed and willing to wave their weapons around. Truly, did you think that little thing was all you needed against me? I'm insulted. Now put it away."

Slowly, he put the knife back into his belt.

"Somewhat better. Do you have a name?"

"No."

"Nothing to put on your tombstone?"

His heart might have skipped a beat.

"What a shame. Perhaps we'll put 'Frog' on your grave."

She was baiting him, with glee.

"Doctor Gantry has left the country?"

"Well, that I cannot answer," Miranda said coyly. "Willful ignorance, you know. If I can't say for certain, then you can ask me all day long and never get an accurate answer. It was planned that way."

The man folded his arms. "I think I know where she's gone. My employer will guess too. You have not really done more than to mildly delay us."

"You employer is only going to know what you told him the last time because you are not communicating with him anymore. And please, do something to make me have to shoot you. I so long to send a message to that horrible man you work for – who thinks he can push my friend and me around – who thinks he can operate with impunity inside the borders of my country."

He tried to look unimpressed. "You will not shoot."

"*Oui*, I will. But I don't think I'll need to just yet. If you want to live," she said, hearing the voices and footsteps just outside her door, "you'll happily go with them. All you may get from them are questions and the boot off our shores. Try anything with me, and I'll – how do the Americans say it – blow your head off."

The housekeeper led the group of British men into Miranda's living room. Everyone except the housekeeper stopped and stared at the gun. The finely dressed man, in charge, pointed to the Frenchman and the fellow was quickly arrested.

Satisfaction played on every aspect of her face as she watched them escort the villain – as she thought of him – away from her home.

"You took away my fun," Miranda declared loudly.

The man in charge stopped. "You wanted to shoot him, Miss Gray?"

"Yes. Don't you, whoever you are?"

He laughed a little.

"Harcourt Lowell, Foreign Office, at your service Miss Gray. And, I have some sympathy for his position."

"I don't!" she quipped and released the hammer on her gun.

"No, I don't expect you do." He finally removed his hat, since he might be there for an extra moment or two. "I'd like to formally thank you for your assistance."

She looked at him, worry now turning her expression. "Do you know how she is doing?"

He nodded. "I can't tell you everything …"

"Of course not."

"… But I can say that she made it safely, has connected as planned with American agents, and remains undetected."

Miranda waved to the chair near him, indicating he could sit.

"I cannot stay. Thank you all the same. My day will now include that rude fellow who burst in here."

"I told you he would do that."

"You did indeed, as did Professor Gantry. I believe we can trust in her instincts from here." When Miranda raised a questioning eyebrow, he continued, "Those instincts may be raw but they have proven effective and reliable so far. She is alive, after all these years."

"You don't know Lettie as I do. But then, you may be quite right." She crossed the room and offered her hand in a very assertive and masculine manner. "It's a pleasure to finally meet you rather than merely sending messages to a name in the Foreign Office. Lettie spoke highly of you."

It was possible Lowell blushed for a moment. "Again, my sincere thanks for the risks you have taken. Will you extend my thanks to Professor Moore as well?"

"Of course."

He stopped and looked back at her. "Miss Gray, should you ever decide the publishing business or your archaeological proclivities are no longer satisfying, I hope you will reach out to me."

"At the Foreign Office? Are you hiring ladies now?"

"More along the lines of accepting volunteers. But my office is not the only place a lady with – such bravery and common sense – can find opportunity. Good day, Miss Gray."

"Mr. Lowell."

She could see what Lettie saw in him. Too bad she knew better than to assume all his colleagues and other spy masters were so charming. Indeed, it would be a cold day in hell before she worked for the government. She preferred by far to offer her services on a case-by-case basis, as she felt reasonable.

Chapter 25

Black Butte, California, United States of America
Stop between Shasta Springs and Berryvale/Sisson

The environment was as unlike Egypt as one could believe, reassuring her that her disdain for the idea of an ancient temple inside the volcano was correct. Lettie stepped off the stagecoach and into the highland forest surrounding the gigantic mountain. Pine trees, thick and aromatic, stretched in all directions. Streams popped and chugged down the slopes of the hillside, dragging brown and red clay with them. Pine cones splintered under her feet or scattered away from the sweep of her foot. Above, far above, two vultures circled with no singular target to focus their efforts. That fact gave Lettie a moment of relief; they hadn't found anything – anyone – to devour.

Yet.

To the west stood the source of the running water, warm springs, and strange weather: Mount Shasta. A skirt of luscious green swathed the lower third of the giant volcano; a blanket of melting snow covered the rest, all the way up to her two peaks. The mountain more than dominated the valley, it caused it to exist and to ever change in a violent setting. Above the fourteen-thousand-foot edifice, the weather swirled and reset to the demands of the alien landscape. Lettie knew the vast differences one encountered at the top of such mountains. The glaciers and blowing snow pack. The broken lava flows. The thin air and blasting winds over two miles above the valley floor.

Stories were told that this beauty had erupted in 1750. No one had confirmed this, but eventually she knew her science would, if she did not herself on this journey. Well, she was here on a fool's errand and might as well put her skills to work. Downstream from the Sacramento River were several growing cities and plenty of farm land. Learning more about the volcano and its dangers was essential to those who might be the first drastically effected.

Lettie watched as the stage driver left her bed-roll and a small trunk by the side of the road. He looked around, his face screwed up with concern. "Ain't no one here."

"There will be. Thank you so much."

He pushed his hat back on his head and stared at the woman. "Listen here, miss. It'll be cold out tonight and there is a small town over that hill. Don't know if they got room but I'm sure someone'll take you in. If you take my advice, head there now. Another stage ain't along until this time tomorrow."

"That's very kind of you, sir. I will take your advice if my friends don't arrive in the next hour."

He nodded and then shook his head.

Such kindness, but he needn't worry about her, she thought. She'd packed light – only the essentials. She'd dressed light: in a thin wool blouse, a smart skirt of ankle length, her sturdy boots, her lava burnt gloves, a wide-brimmed hat, and a long wool cashmere coat that she could practically wrap herself in to sleep outdoors. If it weren't for all the yardage and wool, she might have been mistaken for a seasoned safari guide.

And, she'd slept under the stars before, wrapped in clothing, blankets, and even a bear skin. Out in the cold of Colorado's Estes Park. She'd narrowly escaped two pyroclastic flows, three mad geniuses, and one horrific mud slide. A rough and tumble region of America was no challenge at all.

A moment later, all she could see was the dust from the wheels of the Siskiyou Trail Stagecoach as it rolled down a worn, dark brown road. Looming above the road was a cinder cone she was dying to climb. She had read that it, called Black Butte, was some three thousand feet high, and covered in loose cinder blocks. What a challenge that would be! The stage kept diminishing in size in comparison to the cone until it was a speck on the horizon, following the road to maneuver around the base of it.

A raven began cawing deep inside the forest and she began to notice sets of bright blue birds hopping down to the ground or springing from pine tree to pine tree. The larger of the blue birds had black heads and were particularly aggressive as they came to see if she had anything of interest. Two squirrels chased each other around the trunk of a thick conifer, their claws scratching the bark as they clung to each inch: up and down and up again.

The forest was delightfully alive. In the absence of human activity, nature was thriving quite boisterously. The wind mimicked the rush of a river as it raced through the long needles of the trees. Everything was intensified to her senses. The pine. The rich dirt. The sting of icy breezes. The blue of the sky was brighter. The swirl of the clouds trapped in Shasta's weather hovered over the northwest flank of the volcano.

Suddenly, it was still. The blue jays flew away, the squirrels stopped racing around the tree trunks. Silent.

The ground beneath her feet trembled.

Volcanic earthquake?

Lettie looked to the mountain, but saw nothing to indicate an eruption. That wasn't the only explanation for an earthquake but it was the one that immediately worried her. The tremble became a rumble, then the sound of an engine. It didn't belong there.

Down a side path that cut through the dense forest came a motorized cart. It was ugly, rusted, and ungainly. The small stack on its flank pumped out blackened smoke. Two men with eye protection and bandanas appeared to be controlling it. It was not a motor vehicle like the one her Welsh neighbors had once built. This was something else. A flatbed protruded out the back and flopped along noisily behind.

She stepped out of the road to make way as the whole mechanism plunged down the small embankment and skidded into the ruts made by the stage. The driver glared at her as the vehicle chugged past, but said nothing – acknowledged nothing of the lone woman standing in the middle of nowhere.

She was forced to wave off the pungent smoke, which once it cleared, revealed three more men, on horseback. One had a rider-less, saddled horse in tow. The others had pack mules.

"Professor?" The lead man said, with some disdain.

"Yes."

He looked around her. "No other bags? Trunks. Dresses or luggage?" He seemed confused. "Hat boxes. Women's things?"

"I'm here on a singular mission – a scientific one. I have no need for unnecessaries up here." She picked up her bed-roll, quietly grateful that she might not need it – just because she knew how to sleep in the cold didn't mean she wanted to do so. Anything superfluous had been left back at the Upper Soda Springs Stagecoach Hotel, though perhaps the name was far grander than the accommodation. She marched over to one of the mules before any of the men could dismount and began tying her roll into place. "I'm sure you don't wish to waste time. May I ask who you are?"

"Nobody," the lead man said flatly.

"Don't be ridiculous." Lettie tied down her mad valise behind the bed roll and started back to fetch the small trunk. "You're somebody. Everyone is somebody." Americans, she thought. Not great communicators.

The lead man signaled one of the others to go help her with her trunk. Nonsense. She could lift it. But the younger man, after tipping his hat, politely took the trunk back to the mule he led.

"Well, Mr. Somebody. Can you tell me what that contraption was?" she pointed in the dusty direction the vehicle.

"Nothin' much. Just somthin' some folks put together."

"There's quite a bit of that these days, isn't there?" They must have been surprised when Lettie walked over to the spare horse and mounted rather quickly. She did take advantage of a large bolder but never once gave them a chance to assist her. These were cowboys, she decided, and if everything she'd read about the American Frontier was true, they were not interested in manners or courtesies. Rugged and independent, those were words she saw used repeatedly.

"Ain't got a sidesaddle."

"As you can see, I don't need one, thank you." Her skirt was voluminous enough to split and cover her legs though riding astride. She'd done this before. Frankly, she didn't like to ride astride – and not for silly, prudish reasons – she preferred the comfort and control she'd learned as a little girl riding aside. She said nothing. She'd give these fellows nothing to complain about. This was a game she played every day with men. Confidently, she took up the reigns.

Her horse was a lovely bay mare that seemed just a little bored. It was likely they picked the creature for a temperament that would be suitable for a woman – or rather, a fussy British woman professor. Just as well. She didn't feel up to the task of proving how she could master her ride in addition to everything else. Her head didn't feel right, between the unusual hairstyle and hat – the real necessities, heavy though they were. She reached up to see that none of her hair had shifted and could feel the weight of it. Not wishing to draw attention, she didn't prod it too much.

Slowly, they made their way back into the forest. The path was well worn, both by hooves and wheels. Brown dirt became black as they approached the mountain. On either side were outcroppings of basalt, gray and eternal looking.

A loud clunking sound came from Lettie's trunk. A sound that suggested movement but not breakage.

Mr. Somebody looked back. "What's in that? Don't sound like woman's goods."

"Well, they're this woman's goods. Scientific equipment for testing samples. Notebooks. Reference materials. A microscope and several lenses. A few pieces of climbing gear in case I need to get to an otherwise inconvenient elevation. Base samples. Nitroglycerin …"

His eyes grew wide.

"I'm joking. Nothing liquid is in there except for one, well-sealed bottle of vinegar. As for what you might be suggesting as women's goods, I find them handy for tightly packing and padding delicate equipment. I'm far more concerned with my microscope than any fripperies."

"I thought you were serious for a moment. About the nitro."

"Well, Mr. Somebody, I do think one should employ a sense of humor whenever possible."

He scowled and kept riding. Lettie kept pace behind him, while the others fell slightly behind, but never out of sight.

The ride was not smooth, such as the one she'd taken on Rotten Row in London. The track was not manicured daily – in fact, it was hardly a track at all. Her horse slipped a few times, and bounced as each hoof found different heights in the roadbed. The horses huffed and puffed, somewhat protesting the weight of each rider. Occasionally, the one she rode tried to stumble a bit to one side just to see if it could scrape her off with some low hanging branch. Lettie would duck and reign, and stayed firmly on back.

"Pilser." He said, bluntly after those long, few minutes.

"Pardon me?"

"Pilser. Daniel Thaddeus Pilser."

She thought he rather looked appropriate for the name. He was tall and rail thin. His face was what she had expected: tanned and weathered cruelly. The lines around his eyes and mouth were deep and only expressive when he wanted them to be. His eyes were blue, but not as intense as Turner's were, she noted with some regret. A slate blue. Underneath his hat, his hair was a dulling red with a streak or two of gray. His eyebrows seemed to be knitted permanently together in aggravation or sensitivity to the bright, high-altitude sunlight. Yet, he somehow had a raw sincerity to his existence that radiated out with every gentle correction to his horse or calm response to noise from the brush.

"How do you do, Mr. Pilser."

"Nah. I'm not a "Mister." That's for the bosses. Just call me Pils. Everyone does."

"Oh, I can't do that." She startled him. "Fine British training simply won't let me. You'll just have to put up with my calling you something respectful."

Pils turned away for a moment, entirely thrown off by her lighthearted comments. He looked to be ready to reply when they reached a gully and each rider had to control their descent. Lettie reigned back, discouraging her mare from charging the gully. It was safer for all if neither she nor the horse raced through the ditch.

On the other side of the gully and up a few more yards, she found herself staring at the flank of the volcano. It was exceptionally lovely. Though she knew it was her imagination, she felt it – the power and the weight – the domination of the sky and earth before her. She imagined she could feel the heat of its interior radiating out. Next to them, a little spring bubbled up, producing a tiny amount of steam that disappeared only a foot off the ground. The warm water poured down the hill behind them. Well, she thought, she hadn't been wrong about the heat.

Chapter 26

Montague Hot Springs Ranch
Northeast of Mount Shasta, California

As was expected, her arrival was met with curiosity, welcome, and derision. The "Ranch" was little more than an extremely ornate house for the owner and several simplistic shacks for the workers. Fences and equipment divided the landscape nearly as much as the housing differences. As they came closer, Lettie saw that the shacks weren't too primitive and perhaps weren't hovels after all, yet nothing matched the central house. It was built in the Queen Anne style so popular in America, with a round turret and a porch that skirted the entire home, all the way around. There would never be a time when the view or the sunlight couldn't be changed or followed by simply moving to another spot.

Other cowboys leaned against fences and watched as she rode in, confident in the fact that an Englishwoman could travel anywhere in the world and be relatively safe – mad inventors notwithstanding. A nicely dressed man stepped out of the front door of the house and waited while she dismounted and removed her gloves. He had white hair, thinning at the top, with bushy white eyebrows and long sideburns – equally snowy white.

"Professor. Welcome to Montague Hot Springs. I'm Gregory Jenkins – Geographer. The others are inside and waiting for the opportunity to meet such a distinguished volcanologist." He held out his hand to assist her up the stairs.

She stopped and must have had the most astonished look on her face.

"Ma'am, please do not worry. Only a handful of persons are aware of your presence. You being here is not for public knowledge, I assure you."

Flockmocker's warning about more than two people knowing meant plenty of people knew your secret rang in her hears. "I'm relieved to hear that. I do wish to thank you for indulging me with this little deception."

"I admit I'm curious as to why you are being so close with your cards, as we Yankees like to say."

"My most recent misadventures have brought me so much publicity that I find I cannot do my work without a great deal of interference from well-wishers and critics. The remoteness of this mountain and the quiet will allow me to concentrate. I'm actually re-making my model."

"Truly!" he exclaimed. "I hope you won't mind if this well-wisher," he indicated himself, "asks a few mathematical questions?"

"Not at all."

The interior was sumptuous, in red and burgundy. It was gaudy, as though the owner was wealthy enough not to care what anyone thought of their purchase.

"This is not your home, is it?" she asked.

"On my salary?" he laughed in response.

"Well, I was hoping Americans appreciated their scientists a bit more than Europeans, but alas …"

"Indeed, my dear lady. I fear we will always be underappreciated." He led her to a room filled with a light layer of cigar smoke, the warmth of a roaring fire in the fireplace, a large table with padded chairs, and several gentlemen wearing their opinions on their expressions. Typical, she thought.

"Gentleman," Jenkins began, "I have the pleasure of introducing Professor Letticia Gantry, incognito."

The first man to step forward was an American naval man, and in that moment, Lettie's heart jumped. But no – it was not Tom Turner. "Captain Croft," he said, gently holding out his hand. "I'll be escorting you to British Columbia once we're done here."

She smiled at the short but well-presented man. "You're a bit far inland, aren't you?"

"Born just north of here. I consider this a viable and, if I may say, pleasurable vacation from my normal routines as well as a brief trip home."

Trust absolutely nothing, she heard Lowell's voice clearly in her head. "How kind of you to say." It was rather routine of him to say. The vague comment was purposely masked by the distracting compliment. Very typical. Normally, this ploy was used when a man was avoiding the urge to explain to her that she was out of her league and ought to go home. In this case, she was certain he was keeping the true nature of his business there a secret. Well, it was only fair – she had secrets too.

The next man was clean shaven, and tall. Ruddy skin and dark brown eyes. Dark hair combed over a bald patch at the center of his scalp. "Professor. A pleasure. Zachariah Billings." Billings? Ah, yes, the railroad man mentioned in the dispatch from General Sherman.

Pils quietly opened the door, set her valise inside where she could reach it, and left without a word. For a moment, she was sorry he couldn't stay – grumpy, rough, and unpolished, he struck her as earthy and honest – a considerable difference from the men standing before her.

Finally, a blond but dark eyed fellow resting one arm on the fireplace mantle nodded in her direction, then reluctantly offered his hand after quickly moving a cigar out of it. "Elijah Coleman. I must say I'm not pleased to see a lady travelling to the wilds of America by herself."

"Must you?" she asked, dripping the comment in innocence. "Perhaps I will surprise you. You do like a surprise now and then?"

The other men in the room laughed and Coleman merely produced a slight grin. "Maybe you will."

"Well, thank you all the same," she said in that practiced sort of way, "for being concerned for my welfare, but I have been all over the world and can say for certain that an Englishwoman can go around the globe unscathed. Gentlemen, if you have any questions about my work, I should only be more than happy to answer them. I would not be investing my life in such pursuits were they not exciting to me."

They quickly looked around at one another. Jenkins spoke up first. "Wouldn't you like to rest or refresh yourself first?"

"No need to. I found the ride here very invigorating. There will be time, no doubt, later."

"Very well. Professor, if you would sit here by the fire, I certainly would like to hear about this new model of yours."

Lettie took up her valise, and while walking over to a chair being held for her, noted that the contents of the bag had been shifted and then put back into order – and order was never what she used to organize its contents. It had been searched. No doubt her trunk was being rifled through as they were seated. Her gloves were set on the table but her hat remained on. Good manners allowed her to keep her hat on. And – it was important she not remove it.

She carefully removed a journal and set it in front of her. Slowly, her hands moved over its cover, as though it were an ancient text of the most sacred knowledge. Only then, when she looked up, did she see the newspaper. "May I see that?"

"Only the most upsetting news." The Captain took up the paper before she could reach it. "If I may, I'm sure there are some uplifting articles I could read …"

She looked up angrily. It was a step over the line she'd mentally drawn to distinguish what she would and wouldn't tolerate. "My father never did such a thing when I was young. We learned to accept the good with the bad." She held out her hand – the demand was clear but unspoken. Reluctantly, the Captain handed it to her.

"Her father probably should have," whispered Coleman to Billings. "Damn unnatural."

She heard him. She would have commented, were the news so entirely unacceptable.

"Doctor Jenkins, gentlemen. Have you read this?" When only one of them, Jenkins, nodded, she set the paper down. "I am sorry to begin our afternoon with sad news," Jenkins looked to Lettie, to see if she was at all concerned. "Former President U.S. Grant has passed away."

There was an overall shock and sadness in the room. No one appeared to want to believe it regardless of what the papers said.

Coleman put his cigar down. "Was it the throat cancer?"

Lettie thought it odd that of all the men in the room, the smoker would comment such. But as Jenkins nodded, she watched Coleman push his cigar just a few more inches away.

"Gentlemen, my deepest condolences," she said softly and genuinely. "President Grant was a great soldier and a man of extraordinary integrity, though sometimes he was not surrounded by those of equal measure. I am very sorry to hear this. He is – was – greatly respected by leaders in the Empire."

"Thank you, Professor," Coleman said, obviously pleased by what she said and how she had said it. He didn't know, she was sure, that she meant it, truly.

It took some time for everyone to get arranged at the table. She also thought it likely that they were each gathering their thoughts about the death of Grant and storing them away for another time.

"If you gentlemen don't mind getting started, my time here is limited and I wish to make the most of it."

"Why incognito?" Coleman asked bluntly.

"As you know, I've had a bit much of publicity lately. Contrary to popular opinion, I do not want it, nor have I ever sought it. While I never minded my journalistic efforts being successful, I rather find it upsetting to be further known by the public. The last two years, however, I have failed in my hope to stay out of the public eye. I truly only want to put my scientific knowledge to work. I have some models I'm working on to better predict volcanic activity, a desire to observe new mountains, and perhaps a proclivity to travel. And, if I can also be of assistance to the new railroad line, then I am remarkably happy. Thus, I am here but not here."

She accepted the rolls of maps from Billings. "Best to date, Professor."

"Thank you. I'm quite looking forward to this. And to be clear, once I've headed home, you can announce that I've been here. My hope is that I may, through reputation and hard work, provide you with the data you need to complete your line. I should like it to be the safest and certainly the most efficient route possible."

"No question," the Captain said. "No one seems to know volcanoes as you do."

"I promise not to bore anyone with long tales of rocks and dirt," she smiled as they laughed.

"Heaven's no. We would never miss out on an opportunity to dine with a lady of such note. You must promise to tell us about the East Indies and Krakatoa."

I shall have to skip telling you about the bodies, she noted sadly while pretending to demur. Such information tended to quell the feelings of excitement about an exotic volcano and to accentuate the need for compassion for those lives lost.

Chapter 27

Location Unknown

Yes, it was cold.

He'd been colder by far. As his legs began to shake a bit, and the blanket of lucid sleep began to fall away, he recalled just how much colder he'd been – and when.

He hadn't yet bothered to open his eyes. His lids felt heavier than any other part of his body.

He hurt. His back and ribs burned, yet somehow they weren't broken. He knew what broken bones felt like. His face had been struck, not by the cudgel, but by a fist. Well, nothing was likely broken there, either. Bruised and swelling perhaps, but not broken. He could move his jaw and knit his brows together.

And, he had that far too frequent sensation that he was going nowhere quickly. His right wrist was sore, hefty, and feeling entirely alien to his arm. Oh, yes, he knew that feeling too. Thick, iron manacles felt just like that. He knew from experience.

Tom Turner listened for several minutes. All he could hear was a hollow wind blowing in the distance and his own heartbeat. If such a thing were truly possible, he felt the air around him in a rather implausible attempt to sense if someone or something was near him. It was a matter of perception and old habit. Was there a movement of air across his skin or was that the remnant of the distant wind?

At one point, Turner reminded himself, his senses would overreact to the slightest minutia. He heard nothing moving and felt no one near.

It was cold. Wherever he was, it was not on board the *Master of the World*. On the ground, or under it. Not buried – perhaps in a cave. Or a tunnel! Of course, he had seen the volcano before he'd passed out in pain and exhaustion. Was this a lava tube, such as those he encountered in the Kingdom of Hawaii?

Still keeping his eyes closed, he mentally reviewed his whole being. Head hurt but that was certainly to be expected. Odd, but welcome. Dead men can't feel anything. Had he been drugged – it hadn't left a lingering effect. Welcome again. His face didn't hurt as much as he would have expected, even with the several punches he had taken. All in all, it could have been worse.

His left hand. That was beginning to throb a bit, but he could feel a bandage around it, and it was not manacled. To prove it to himself, he lifted his arm up and touched his face. Bandage. Unchained. A kind gesture considering the foolishness of the way he'd used his left fist – he was lucky his fingers weren't broken. Now he could remember. They'd thought he was unconscious from the beating. He'd tried to escape when they were taking him back to the dark room. Not his brightest decision. Still, in the heat of the fight, misjudgments are prone to happen.

Turner was on his back, laid out on something hard and flat. He drew his legs up, tenderly, and was pleased to find that they too were unfettered. Only his right wrist was chained.

Robur could have done so much more to beat or drown him into submission. Why hadn't he? Because Turner was his "Tom," and Robur had stayed his hand. He wouldn't do that a second time if Turner failed to give him what he wanted.

It was time to sit up, but his heavy eyes simply didn't want to cooperate. Neither did his back. Could have been so much worse.

So, Turner decided, he was on some sort of table, set up in a makeshift holding cell, in a lava tube, inside the volcano. Which volcano, he wasn't sure but he suspected that it was Mt. Shasta. Chained by one wrist, to keep him restrained but not unable to move relatively comfortably. The drug was mild. He'd even been given some medical aid.

Oh, yes, that would-be Robur – though more like the Robur he'd known before.

Trying to sit up was harder than he'd expected. He settled back down on the table and began rubbing his eyes with his free hand.

At least he doesn't know where the object or the scroll are, Turner thought with satisfaction. The statue portion was far away, safe in England. Lettie Gantry had probably hidden it deep in some box, in some closet, on the campus of New College of London. He'd called it a "Key." Robur would want and need both parts.

His eyes opened! He had lied, under torture, where he'd sent the Key. What if Robur had found it – with Lettie – and had left him behind while he went to retrieve it? He had threatened to kill her.

No, he thought. It wasn't possible. He had to believe the Key was far away, where Robur wouldn't know to look. Lettie would hide it: she was brilliant. She was equal to Robur, most especially in his current state, but truly at any time. She surrounded herself with equally brilliant people, himself excluded, he added as a reminder to his occasionally arrogant internal voice. Besides, Robur was sure that the Key was sent to Hetzel, so his focus would be on getting Turner to tell him about the other half, about the Scroll.

Was Lettie safe at all? It seemed that Robur hadn't started his reign of terror across the ocean yet. That might give him time to find a way to protect her. Before he could feel guilt for having involved her, he reminded himself that she was a target long before any Relic had been found.

He squinted and then shut his eyes. There was one lantern, lit. Chemical type. That was thoughtful. Why? Because ultimately, Robur would want to forgive Turner for his errors and draw him back into the fold. He'd always done that. In the entire time he'd known Robur, he'd been the balance against the Captain's rash behavior – and that sometimes meant disobeying or countermanding him. Every time, Robur would voice his displeasure, warn Turner not to do that again, and go on as if nothing had happened. Turner always suspected that Robur was grateful for the efforts to keep him from completely fouling things up. Not that the Captain could ever admit it, but Turner had more recently decided that it was his own reputation for breaking the rules that had caused Robur to seek him out in the first place.

Turner opened his eyes again.

The lantern gave the place a warm glow – which made it all the more confusing. Made it worse.

His eyes were wide and his thoughts stopped for a moment, before racing into every scenario he could come up with to explain …

To explain?

What was going on?

Lying on his back, he found himself staring up at the bottom of a carved figure's head. Long, stretching out from the body, carefully cut from the hardened lava – a feat that was remarkable in itself. Turner shifted his body, as much as the chain on his right wrist would allow. With the light, he could see that it was a statue standing over him. Stiff in its pose. It was huge. It filled the whole height of the lava tube.

Yes, a lava tube. He was right about that.

He stared at the statue. Left foot extended in front of the body. Arms straight down at its sides, rounded into fists. One fist held an object he'd seen before but couldn't quite place. It appeared to be wearing a tight-fitting shirt and a kilt. Care had been given to the details of its wide, flat, jeweled collar; the pattern of the shirt; the pleats of the kilt. Above him, it was the bottom jaw of a canine's snout. Some small patches of light managed to make it to the exceedingly tall and narrow dog ears.

On wobbly legs, Turner climbed off the table – no, it was a box or …

Or a sarcophagus: a coffin. Maybe an altar?

His heart was pounding.

Slowly, Turner moved around the right side of his temporary bed, and stood up.

The statue was designed with the body of a man but the head of a dog. No – a jackal. Turner had seen something like it before. In a museum.

The lantern light also exposed elements on the statue that weren't on those he'd seen in the museum: tubes. Hydraulic lines, just like Robur had. Just like those Turner had seen on Hetzel's biomechanical monsters. Just like those on the Relic.

The statue wasn't the only one.

If only the lantern light could shine that far.

He knew what he'd see: ten, twenty, maybe a hundred more ancient, animistic gods. In rows. Cut into and out of the lava. Disappearing into the unlit expanse.

Primal terror. Horrible, lonely, and beyond reason. Turner's mind kept seeing movement in the distance; kept hearing scratching and scattering sounds. His mind was playing tricks on him. The harder he looked, the more imaginary things he was sure he was seeing.

He shut his eyes and rattled the chain on his wrist, both to reestablish his sense of reality.

Please God, he thought, not entirely understanding the gut feeling of abject terror, *keep Lettie and that Key far from here*. He didn't know why, but he knew – he knew! – Keep the Relic away from Robur and – and *this* place!

The wind kept howling in the distance.

The lantern flickered.

As far away from here as possible!

Lettie looked at her trunk. Yes. It too had been searched. Closing the curtains on her window and stepping back out of the light, she carefully unrolled her hair. The device slipped out of the long strands of black hair, snagging only slightly as it dropped into her hand. Small but heavy. She would be fighting a headache until this business was done.

If the general mumble she heard coming from downstairs was any indication, nothing urgent was on their minds or in their conversation. That was good.

She looked at the relic – the device, she preferred to call it. It was a key, but to what exactly? Or simply a schematic? How old was it really?

She wanted to be so angry at Turner for involving her, but she wasn't. Tired enough to sleep without any difficulty, she knew she couldn't – time was of the essence. Robur had Tom, but where? How long would it take for Robur to break him? What was he doing to …

She had to admit it; she was here to save Tom. The Relic and the potential for an ancient site were both intriguing. The chance to explore a new volcano was exciting. Perhaps even the possibility to beat Hetzel at his own game was deeply satisfying. She'd give that all up to find Tom, alive and well.

Slowly, she began brushing her hair, which felt thinner but strong. There was no mirror in the room. Probably a good thing. She no doubt looked a bit worn, but the last few weeks had been more than trying. Deep down, she couldn't help but think this was all about to become something either quite different or quite resolved. The latter was definitely appealing. Once she'd finished brushing, she braided all her hair into one long plait, then coiled it into a high chignon – burying the device underneath.

Chapter 28

Montague Hot Springs, Mt. Shasta, California

She was very underdressed for dinner. How odd, she mused, that she was admonished for potentially bringing too many items of clothing – which she did not – while the men were lauded for bringing formal dinner wear to the countryside. There they all were: black ties, waistcoats, and two of them in tails. The Captain was in his Mess Dress uniform. She, on the other hand, was now un-dusted and tidied up.

The conversation, over a splendid roast with potatoes and corn, was nothing of any importance – to any of them.

To Lettie, it was a chance to see who each man really might be. The Captain was very interested in his appearance, always keeping his needed reading glasses hidden as much as possible. Billings was a dandy, or at least in his own mind. He was fancier than the others, but then, it was likely that he had the funds to be such. Coleman kept giving her the eye, in that it seemed he just couldn't accept her as anything but an ornamental dinner companion. Jenkins kept his face and conversational topics quite neutral.

Each of them was supposed to be wholly ignorant of the real reason she was there. What if they were not who they claimed to be? How would she know? How could she tell? Perhaps it was a paranoia generated by the books she'd been reading of late, but she was quite convinced that at least one of them was a spy for Robur or Hetzel.

No, that was too much nonsense. She needed to deal in facts.

Interestingly, Jenkins appeared to be running out of the energy to stay awake. Billings was almost too energetic, yet his enthusiasm was directed at the drawings. If he was part of the attacks, he was making no effort to hide his interests. Coleman was growing argumentative – something she was sure meant he was hiding behind his opposition to anything Billings said.

Pils and a few men had also been invited to the table, ostensibly to fill it out. He wasn't entirely uncomfortable, but suggesting that he liked dining in such a manner would have been challenged by his somewhat brow-beaten expression. He was there as decoration, not as an actual guest. Jenkins never directed a question toward him nor even looked at him.

She felt a bit sorry for him. Desperately, she wanted to ask him what he knew about the land around the mountain, best places to look for geologic evidence such as outcroppings, obsidian, or cooled lava rock. She couldn't. A balance had been achieved by all the players and if she was to observe their behavior, then she could not upset that balance.

"Glass Mountain," Jenkins said, catching her attention. "It is south from here, but they say you can find obsidian if you look for it."

"That speaks volumes for the sort of volcano it is. I would expect there to be signs of rhyolite and other types of lava flows. Perhaps even pyroclastic evidence."

"We seem to only have granite around here, though they say there are sides of the mountain you can pick up obsidian everywhere."

She set her fork down. "I was looking at your map of the river valley approaching this region. On my way here, I noted some rather spectacular cliffs to the west. Castle Craig."

Billings leapt in. "Glorious edifice. It will make a brilliant tourist stop on our line."

Lettie quickly considered her words. "They looked to be a rather challenging climb. Your average tourist might not be able to make that ascent."

"I'm sure there will be tours up the mountain too."

Jenkin added, "A pair of ladies managed it in 1856. Miss Harriette Eddy and Mary McCloud. Summited and returned without a scratch. Colleagues of yours, Professor?" He kept using her title as if it were quaint.

"I'm afraid I do not know them. But I suspect their adventures will encourage a trend amongst tourists. I should only hope no one underestimates the environment. It has been my observation that those who do not respect the mountain they are climbing will likely fall afoul of it – sometimes with a loss of life."

The Captain looked up. "I do believe this is where we ask about Krakatoa."

Of course. She had a well-practiced routine of properly crafted stories. Refusing to leave off descriptions of the true disaster and death toll, she told the shocking details and adventures to her willing audience, occasionally slipping in a bit of geologic science where she could.

Pils sat almost enraptured by it all. When Coleman made a quip about dead natives, Pils did not laugh as the other men did. She caught a sympathetic glance from the cowboy, as though he understood she neither liked speaking about death nor laughing at other's tragedies.

Outside, while the rich men were smoking and drinking and everyone was sure she'd gone to her room like a proper lady, Lettie walked out onto the porch. It was a beautiful evening, with enough moonlight to provide a sheen on the thick snowfall blanketing the mountain. Some cloud formations were hovering above the summit, but otherwise the air was crisp and clear. A strong breeze whipped through the trees and scattered the ever-present pine needles across the hard-packed earth.

Off toward the north end of the ranch's living area was a simple, newly painted building. Lights shone out into night, followed by laughter and fiddle music. One of the ranch hands knew how to play.

Something howled in the distance, far enough to be heard but not threatening. Likely, no animal would venture into the houses. Yet, there must be tempting scraps for the smarter and faster creatures. Certainly, not every bit of food presented at dinner was consumed. The ranch hands likely wouldn't like the gesture of being given the leftovers but there was a staff in the big house. Even with all that, surely a place this filled with human activity would have plenty of human garbage for an eager raccoon to pick through.

Horses huffed and shuffled around, but nothing to indicate a sense of fear on their part. Two of the horses were saddled. Perhaps someone was going on a night patrol. A wolf or coyote howled in the distance. A dog barked on the far side of the enclosure. Wagons creaked as the wind rocked them gently back and forth.

It was the West – the Wild, Untamed West.

She had to try *it* – the little vice.

On the belief that she would find *him*, she had taken the liberty of purchasing a half dozen sweet cheroot cigarillos. She'd never tried such a thing, but women were starting to smoke – in public too. It was exotic and scandalizing. She pulled the one she brought down from her room out of her coat pocket, along with a match and book. This was all very new and reasonably exciting. She would never be able to smoke one of those horrid cigarettes everyone seemed to be rolling and then puffing. They simply stank. But the cigarillo was much more like pipe smoking. A more perfumed smoke.

There was of course the rumor that such smoking was related by President Grant developing throat cancer. She would try this but not make it a habit.

How Turner would probably laugh at her. Heavens, if she'd married him, he could order her to stop. That was an uncomfortable thought. Still, Turner was nowhere around. He thought she was either back in England or in some library trying to figure out what the object was. Either way, he didn't expect her to be where she was. Perhaps he was being kind, staying away, as she hadn't answered his proposal. A lack of answer was an implied "no."

The solid mass of the mountain, all alone in the middle of the plain – it was lonely. So was she. But she accepted the absolute fact that adventure and discovery were enough to counter any longing. Besides, there were other men in the world.

She began to chew a little on one end, to nip it off.

"It's a little easier with this, Professor." Pils walked out of the main doorway to hand her a small cigar cutter. "You don't strike me as a lady who smokes."

"I don't. But I would like to see what this is like. And I seem to be in a place where boorish rules of society are commonly bent to suit."

Pils simply raised an eyebrow. "Do you know what you're doing?"

"No," she said quite honestly. "Much is easy to figure out. Clear the ends so the air and heat can flow through. Don't burn your fingers."

"Don't inhale." He smiled slightly.

"As one shouldn't with a regular cigar?"

He only nodded.

Lettie cut off both ends, handed back the cutter to Pils, and struck the match. A light breeze was blowing and Pils held up his cupped hands to protect her match from being blown out.

Interesting. So close to him now, she could smell that he had bathed as the light scent of soap lingered on his hands. Indeed, she could see his hair now was clean and combed, and he'd taken the time to shave. If by any chance it was for her sake he'd done this, she was flattered. If not – well, the world certainly didn't revolve around her. In the glow of the match, she could see him looking at her – his big, dark, steel-blue eyes.

The cheroot taste was acidic and she immediately knew why it would be a poor decision to inhale. The smoke inside her mouth was strong and sweet – the smoke outside was quite like the pipe Kit Moore occasionally indulged. Balancing the cigarillo between her index and middle fingers, she delicately sampled the cheroot. Pils lit one of his own – a long, moist, dark tube of hastily rolled tobacco. At least there wouldn't be a stench from dried tobacco in one of those cigarettes.

"Professor, may I ask a question?" He leaned against the porch railing.

Lettie nodded.

"What made you become a …" he searched for the word. "What we call a dirt sniffer, if you'll excuse the rude term."

"I enjoy geology." She kindly handed him the word he was looking for.

"Yes, ma'am. But why become a professor? Why geology? Why volcanoes?"

"One damn near killed me," she said, wondering if he'd react to her swearing. He didn't seem to. Her experiment in free living was going rather well. "I was a child and I was caught in a mud flow after an eruption, in the East Indies. Wiped out a great many people. So, I decided right there and then, no regular life for me. I want to see if I can save people."

He looked at her as though she were an object in some museum. "How would you do that?"

"Mathematics. Statistics. Formulas. Research." Clearly, he wanted to understand but didn't yet. "I once thought I could create a simple equation that could be used to predict every single volcanic eruption in the world. Such a prediction could save tens of thousands of lives, by evacuating villages, diverting potential floods, and other such ideas. I was wrong."

"Do other scientists say that sort of thing: 'I was wrong?'"

Lettie shrugged. "Some do. But my goal isn't getting my name on some discovery. As a woman, I daresay I don't expect to be given credit for anything at all. But I know what one volcano – one eruption can do."

Pils waited. "Doc Jenkins says you were at Krak-a-tow? The big volcano in the Orient?"

Lettie smiled. "I was there, yes. I saw it erupt and once again, a volcano bloody near got me. And those who didn't escape – well, that was rather horrible. I don't believe I've seen anything quite that bad. Yet," she looked at him comfortably, "Krakatoa wasn't really such a big volcano, though you wouldn't know it by the size of the eruption. And the devastation it caused."

"You think that mountain up there could erupt bigger?" he indicated with his cigar the lingering light on the summit of Shasta.

"That's what I want to find out."

"And of course you're not here because of all the strange goings-on?" There was a tone of incredulousness in his voice.

"Have there been people coming all that way to see some sensationalized rubbish?"

"We've had plenty of tourists. Most go home disappointed. Are you here for those stories too?"

"Stuff-and-nonsense if you ask me. I was reading about those on my way here. I thought about going home or picking another volcano to do my research, just to avoid any sensationalized drivel." She didn't like lying to him, but it was necessary. "Though, I do suspect that my colleagues informed Dr. Jenkins and the others that I was coming – so that they might keep an eye on me. Very flattering, but I also give little credence to newspaper stories about mysterious lights and strange happenings. I can speak from experience; some newsmen will say anything to sell their papers. Most are honest, but there are those who trade in luridness."

Pils nodded. "Well, as the Doc told us," meaning the ranch hands, she suspected, "to keep an especial eye on things, you may be right about them watching over you."

"And, as I said, I'm very flattered." She drew in another mouthful of smoke and blew it out into the night air, as if this was the most courageous thing she'd done in ages. "Though it's hardly necessary. I'm quite capable of watching out for my own way. I wouldn't have come out here otherwise." Pils appeared to be quite amused.

"Your turn," she said suddenly.

"My turn for what?"

"Who are you and what are you doing at the foot of a fourteen-thousand-foot volcano in California?"

He laughed with a low, gravelly rumble. "Is that how high it is?" Shaking his head, he said, "I'm not entirely sure how I got here. Don't think I ever thought about getting somewhere as much as I just kept going."

"So nothing as grandiose as a plan?"

"Nah. Plans are worthless out here. Too many open spaces you can't see the end of. Too many secrets. Too many surprises." He drew heavily. "When you meet a man, it's his word and his handshake – that's all. Chances are you'll never meet him again. If he does right by you – fine. If he wrongs you – you either have to take your vengeance or let it go. Nothin' for it but living here and now."

"A viable philosophy, to be sure."

"Probably won't work in the cities."

"You'd be surprised, Mr. Pilser."

"Pils – please. We like things friendly here."

She thought about it. Using a person's Christian name was rather intimate. Even her own parents didn't do so, at least not in public. "Lettie," she stated with a feeling of newness. "Please call me Lettie."

The ground began to shake. Lettie knew that feeling. Pils, however, did not appear to. He first backed away from the railing, as if it was all that was shaking. Looking at her with wide gray eyes, he seemed to ask what the hell was going on. The rumble was under their feet. Small stones began to bounce with the quaking.

"The mountain? Is it erupting?"

Lettie looked out at what was still visible. "No. I don't think so. This isn't an earthquake. It's something heavy – huge …" She started out into the yard, looking for that vehicle she'd seen earlier – when she'd first arrived. The ground shook then too, but not nearly as much. It certainly wasn't an earthquake; the shaking was too steady and even. Earthquakes were random, uneven, and jarring.

Lights flooded the house, causing both Lettie and Pils to shade their eyes. The roar of an engine was terrible and made them both step back. A cloud of dust exploded from the ground, showering them with particles of soil and whatever else had been there.

As quickly as the tumult started, the machine that caused the disturbance arrived. Had she not looked, she would have missed it entirely.

It raced into the yard, suddenly arching toward the sky, and leaving a trail of pungent smoke in its wake. Momentum alone must have lifted it back into the air at an astonishing speed. Wings – she saw wings. Not flapping, but rigid. The body was bird-like though she couldn't quite pick out details.

She didn't need to.

She knew this vessel.

She'd seen one just like it before – in the East Indies.

Despite Pils's protest, Lettie ran through the middle of the yard to look at the thing as it flew away. The smoke lingered but the vessel didn't. She wished the house lights were off. If anything, she might be able to track it as its body in shadow blotted out the stars or a distant set of clouds. Pils kept calling out to her, before finally rushing to her side and grabbing her by the waist.

"Mr. Pilser," she pushed away. "Did you see it? It could fly – some sort of aero-craft – did you see it?"

He looked quite astonished. "See what? I didn't see nothin'."

"It was fast, but I know what I saw."

Other ranch hands had raced out of the bunk house, some in little more than a union suit, but each of them clutching their side arms. There was plenty of cussing and cursing – most had no idea a lady was present. Lettie certainly didn't care if they knew she was there or not.

"You think that was some sort of wagon or..." Pils couldn't find the words.

"Aero-craft sir. It flies."

"It only rolls as far as I can tell," he responded, pointing to a short pair of tracks scratched across the scoured dirt. "Was it moving too fast for us to see?"

The question was surprising. While the idea that any vehicle could move faster than the human eye could perceive might be plausible, it was a remarkable question from a cowboy in the middle of nowhere. It was also remarkably accepting of him that such a possibility existed in the first place.

"Mr. Pilser. If you know to ask that question, I must suspect that you are holding back on …"

The gentlemen of the house raced down the porch and out into the open yard. "What happened here? Pils?"

Pils looked at them, at Lettie, and then at the gentlemen again. Several cowhands were waiting to see what he said. "A quake maybe. Nothing to worry about, sir." He then turned to Lettie with an expression that begged her to say nothing more.

"Professor Gantry. You're our expert – was that an earthquake?"

Pils's eyes were downright pleading.

"It could be," she replied, somewhat truthfully. "I should prefer to inspect things in the morning – when there is light. I simply cannot examine anything in this darkness."

"Will it happen again?" the Captain asked.

"I don't think so. That was rather small by comparison to other earthquakes I've endured." That much was quite true. "I'm sure Dr. Jenkins will share an interest with me in the morning." Jenkins nodded in agreement. "Until then, I think the worst is over and we can all go to sleep comfortably. This region is prone to shaking. Quite average."

The gentlemen looked somewhat relieved. Except for Billings. "Is this the sort of thing I'm supposed to build my line over?"

"If you build wisely, you shouldn't have too many problems. Would you like to discuss it in the morning?" Lettie smiled.

Billings shook his head and walked back into the house, followed by the others. The ranch hands all grumbled until Pils ordered them back into the bunk house.

Once the yard was theirs alone, Lettie turned to Pils. "The lot of you should be used to this sort of thing, considering where you live."

Pils shook his head and stared out toward the mountain. "There haven't been any serious quakes since we got here. And frankly, Lettie, the lot of us haven't been here all that long. The gentlemen got here first." Finally, he looked at Lettie. "I suspect you're wondering why I didn't encourage ya'll to speak more."

"I am curious."

"It's these strange doings. We've been hearing from the town folks all winter that they would hear something – the ground would shake – lights – then nothin'. The gents – they just dismiss it. I didn't think you wanted them making fun of you."

She felt quite soft toward him. "Thank you. Now, will you please – Pils – tell me what you've experienced."

He held up a match, tempting her to relight her cigarillo. "Exactly what you just did, only I swear I never saw what made all the fuss. Just the shaking, the noise, the lights – not what you saw. Not what you recognized. Care to tell me what you thought that was?"

Could she trust him? In some ways, he reminded her of an unpolished version of Tom Turner. And, well, she knew where her trust in him had gone. Though, if she was still angry with Turner, she had decided her righteous indignation weighed less than finding him alive. Pils was honest and forthright. She admired it. But …

"I saw something strange a couple of years ago – in Baltimore. I was absolutely convinced it was a flying craft. Then it was proven not to be. But I do swear I saw something back then." She walked up to Pils to accept the match. "Please don't tell anyone I said something in the heat of the moment. I still have nightmares about Baltimore. It would be very embarrassing …" She smiled at him. "I think all the sensational stories are getting to each of us."

I'm an idiot, she thought almost out loud. *I nearly let someone know how much I'm aware of. Damn it! I know better.*

She sat down on her bed, the springs creaking, and rubbed the back of her neck. The artifact was causing her head to and neck to hurt.

She would need to trust someone. Pils was a likely candidate for that trust, though she had to do so with greater caution. She trusted too easily. That was how Turner had deceived …

She threw back the covers and decided that tonight she should sleep fully dressed. Boots too. It was cold and the extra layers of clothing would help but she needed to be ready to move.

Pils – Daniel Thaddeus Pilser – was keeping a secret from her. He had asked a rather insightful question that she neither hinted at nor was obvious in the heat of the moment.

Footsteps outside her door reminded her of another time someone was stalking her. Before she could think of the many possibilities, there was a low rap on her door. She wrapped her shoulders in a blanket to hide the fact she was still dressed and put the covers loosely back into place. Her valise was quickly in reach.

Lettie opened the door slightly, placing her body in such a way that an attempt at forced entry would be difficult – at first. She had no illusions about her being able to fight her way out of a situation.

Was she in a situation?

Pils was standing near the door. He looked at her, clearly embarrassed. "A moment of your time, please. I'm very sorry. I don't do this sort of thing. We never have women up here and I swear I don't …"

"It's late Pils."

"This is important." His expression began to show a dreadful mix of fear and concern. He pushed his way in with a multitude of apologies, and she let him by, then quickly closed the door behind him, after checking the hallway. "There are lights – up on the mountain. It's best if you don't leave your room."

"Is anyone going up to look?"

His astonished expression told her the answer was no. In fact, she was beginning to think she could hold an entire conversation with whatever emotion played out on his face. He was likely a very poor whist or poker player. "We've seen this sort of thing before. No one wants to volunteer. It'll pass." He walked partially to the window, enough to look out.

"It hasn't so far, if the papers are to be believed."

Turning toward her, he removed his hat and lowered his head, in a deliberate act of submission and contrition. He certainly didn't appear to be aggressive. But then, he drew an Army Colt .44 from his vest.

Lettie drew in a deep breath and reached for the valise at the foot of the bed. She could use it as a weapon if needed.

It was not needed. Holding one finger to his lips, Pils offered her the grip of the Colt. Whispering, he said, "I think you should have this." She took it gently, assuming that he'd loaded it already. "I'm sorry if I gave you a fright, but this is the first time the strange goings-on came this close to the ranch. They've always been somewhere – over there. I don't like it. I've put six bullets in there – smokeless cartridges. I suspect you know how to use it. Now is the time to tell me if you don't."

Lettie held the Colt in both hands, shifted the lock, rolled the cylinder into her palm, then back into the gun. She then locked it back into place, eschewing the nonsense move of spinning the cylinder and clicking the hammer. She'd done it to prove to him she knew the weapon. There was no guarantee that she could hit anything with it, no doubt in his mind, but at least she was unlikely to shoot herself.

"Thank you, Pils."

"Professor. Lettie. I have no idea what's going on out there or even if you've been dragged into this by accident, but there's bizarre things happening around here. Ain't got nothin' to do with volcanoes or ranching. As you and I have come to first names, I can't stand by and see you hurt if I can help you defend yourself accordingly. I don't think you should worry needlessly. This is just to be safe. I ain't sure what's going on or if there is any danger – though after tonight, I just ain't sure."

She waited for a moment while wrestling with her inner voices about what she should or shouldn't do next. Holding tightly to the pistol, she looked up at Pils through her eyelashes. Her eyebrows pressed together and she expected that he would recognize her determination in her expression. "Mr. Pilser, you are very surprising. You've brought me a weapon, which means you are absolutely convinced that I'm in danger. You're not uncertain about it at all. Which makes me wonder; I'm just a silly geologist, poking around a rather large mountain. What possible danger could I be in or pose to someone causing 'bizarre things' to happen?"

"You knew it was a flying machine. You knew awfully fast," he said bluntly, "which makes me wonder if you know more than you're sayin'."

"You knew to ask if it could move faster than human perception. I suspect you're not telling me everything."

"I ain't hiding nothin'."

She tilted her head, as if to see him differently. "Ain't? Nothin'? Weren't? I daresay you are a far better spoken man than that."

He seemed to be flattered by her comment. "Not around here, I ain't." He examined the floor boards for a moment. "My mother was an honest woman who wanted as much as she could get for her only surviving son. She made sure I could read and speak well. But around here, a man has to fit in. That's how it works."

"And your question this evening?" Damn it, now she really liked him. He was taller than her and certainly stronger physically. But there he was, keeping his body purposely in a manner most unlike an aggressor. He was doing his best to be someone she could count on being safe – trustworthy.

"You ever read books that aren't about science?"

"I enjoy a good novel, Mr. Pilser."

"Ever read Jules Verne?"

I've lived a Verne novel, she thought. "Why yes, I rather like his work."

"Me too. Whatever you do, don't tell the boys I have a few of those books under my bunk. Those are the kind of books that give a man ideas – about science and inventions." He smiled with a very warm grin. "Please trust me. And keep that knowledge close. It takes a man a while to build trust out here – and the boys trust me because I don't try to be better than them. It's important." His voice was pleading. There was a need to be accepted – it fit in – and she understood it better than he'd know.

She couldn't trust him entirely and the new state of her life infuriated her. She was beginning to like Pils and his forthright presence. She wanted desperately for him to be her friend and confidant. But she couldn't. Experience told her, go slowly.

"Pils ..."

"Lettie. Ya'll need to be safe. Put that under your pillow." When she nodded in agreement, he continued. "I don't sleep in the big house. Not my place. But if you need me, you shout. I'll come to you, I promise. I won't ever leave a lady to danger – not even a cigarillo smoking lady geologist." His smile was infectious, but he maintained the submissive pose for her comfort. "I don't trust most folk, and like fewer. And I can say for certain that I never met no lady who was half as smart or civil. And you have been very civil to me, despite a rough beginning and you having no reason to concern yourself with a ranch hand. I don't claim to be anything but."

"Yet, you are a natural gentleman, and I thank you for your care. I promise I will keep this with me and do as you suggest." She didn't want to appear smitten or foolish, but she wanted nothing less than to assure him he'd won her affection, however small or limited as it might be by the situation at hand. She offered him her hand – American style. "Thank you, Pils. I promise not to say anything about your reading materials. I think I'll sleep better now."

"No more nightmares about Baltimore?"

"No more nightmares about Baltimore."

Chapter 29

Montague Springs,
Mt. Shasta, California

She knew how to saddle a horse from watching it being done, which meant she was probably going to make a few mistakes. At first, her little mare held its breath, to keep her from tightening the girth too much. Lettie had seen that happen before, and once the mare let her breath out, she quickly tightened it again.

A rifle was nothing difficult to find inside the house. It was a Winchester and reminded her of the Henry she had lost. Ammunition was not difficult to locate either. She'd taken advantage of the fact that few were awake at such an early hour.

She picked up the belt, and made sure that the holster rested in a viable position in front of her left hip, handle turned so that she could easily draw it across with her right hand, military fashion. On the right side of the belt, she'd wedged in her pick hammer. The rifle was loaded and slipped into a holster in the saddle. The wonderful, almost iconic valise she carried everywhere had to be left behind. A blanket, and some jerky from the kitchen, were settled in behind her seat. Water would not be a problem in the area. Lettie pulled her hat down onto her head and pulled the strap tightly under her chin. The lamb's wool coat would be sufficient in the summer nights, as were the wool felt leggings. A simple blouse, waistcoat, and mid-calf split skirt completed a practical set of clothes that would have appalled her mother. Glasses, notebook and pencil, compass, and a magnifying lens. There was no telling how long she would be gone.

The beaded bracelet on her left wrist scratched a bit. It had been a while since she'd worn it. A remnant of her childhood and the promise she'd made to find a way to predict volcanic eruptions. Lettie hadn't fulfilled that promise – yet. All her work on a mathematical equation was proving that such a model couldn't work. When she got back to London, she'd start again. For now, what kept her from feeling overwhelming guilt was that she was keeping a portion of her promise – she would protect those who had no idea what was coming. This was now a matter of semantics, yet she felt justified.

Someone up at the house would be angry to learn that a weapon, bullets, and a horse were gone. She wasn't stealing, not in the literal sense. They were supposed to supply those things for her – in theory.

Taking her ride out the back of the stable, she found herself in pitch darkness. Howling creatures and hooting owls were disturbing but wouldn't stop her.

Outside, she could see precisely what was bothering everyone.

In the distance, portions of the mountain were illuminated by a deep green glow from the Shastina side. The glow moved, changed, brightened, then dulled – then the entire process started again. Low, growling echoed through the air. It was eerie and somewhat otherworldly. Could a natural geologic event explain it? Not one that she could think of immediately.

As she used a hay bale to help her mount, she concluded that this was a man-made phenomenon. Man-made, she repeated silently. Thanks to Hetzel, she knew which man was possibly responsible.

An ancient temple? Unlikely, though sitting staring at ghostly lights moving around the volcano, she didn't feel the confidence she once had. A Relic that Hetzel and others wanted, hidden in her hair, of all insane places. Bio-mechanical monsters. Attacks on scientists. A vehicle that moved so quickly it escaped human detection until the damage it inflicted had been done.

Too bad Pils wasn't with her, but she trusted no one. She rather liked Pils too. He'd be an excellent companion, were this not a mission of secrets, lies, and fiends. Unfairly, he was loosely entangled in the matter, but with enough room to walk away should things become too dangerous or volatile.

Slowly, she walked her horse to the far side of the ranch. She was lucky, there was a break in the fence.

From there, she was on her own.

Robur was on the loose, she thought as the mare stumbled along the grassy hill. Hetzel was determined to control all bio-mechanics.

And Tom Turner was missing – very likely being held by Robur.

Temple or no temple. Monsters or no monsters. She was going to the volcano.

Far from the lights of the ranch, she found a road with the little lantern she carried. The road was narrow and not well used, but a couple of ruts suggested that strange machine from the ranch might have come along there from time to time.

Temples. Monsters. Tom. And a volcano.

It felt oddly familiar as she spurred her mare into a canter.

COMING SOON

Read the New Serial

Automatons of Thebes

Professor Gantry to the Rescue
By T. E. MacArthur
Do Not Miss It

COMING SOON

NEWS OF THE DAY

The Hamburg American Company's new areo-liner Imperator will fly on May 7 on her maiden voyage to New York. The Imperator is the largest passenger dirigible in the world. She is a floating palace 919 feet long, with engines of 80,000 horsepower. She can accommodate 50 passengers. Among other luxuries the Imperator is fitted with a theatre, a restaurant, baths, and private sleeping quarters. The first-class dining saloon is in the Louis XVI style.

Despite the tremendous combined efforts of the American Federal Police, Britain's Scotland Yard and Special Branch, and Iceland's Police services, the whereabouts of the man once known as the Earthshaker remain unknown. The disturbed individual who claimed responsibility for a series of earthquakes in England has disappeared as quickly as he appeared on the scene. The public is assured that the investigation will continue

Attacks in America's heartland continue. According to witnesses, the craft causing such disturbances is rarely seen. Dr. T. Bendix of the University of California, claims that the vehicle moves at no less than 200 miles per hour, a speed at which no human eye may follow it. Dr. Bendix believes the craft to be of "foreign" origin and likely the efforts of a European power seeking retribution for prior offenses. He went on to suggest that the British Empire was seeking to reclaim lands in North America. Mr. H. Lowell, of the Foreign Office, responded absolutely that no official of the Empire was involved with such behavior and suggested that Dr. Bendix was not a doctor at all nor was his sanity to be considered stable.

With significant regret, New College of London has announced the retirement of one of its most beloved professors. Prof. Christopher Moore, of the Archaeological and Anthropological School, has decided that this is an excellent opportunity to take up gentlemen's delights, such as fishing and painting, at his ancestral home in Kent. Students expressed great disappointment. No further comments were offered by the educational institution.

His Imperial Highness, Kaiser Wilhelm I, has instituted significant changes within the Prussian Empire intended to assuage the fears of his neighbors that Prussia intended to start a war across Europe. He has appointed his son, Crown Prince Frederick, as Vice Chancellor to the aging Bismark. The Crown Prince is well known for his humane behavior in times of war and his Progressive ideals – a counterpoint to Bismark's policies. Also appointed was one Karl Franz Nikolaus von Hagen, Admiral, as Chief Minister of the Imperial Prussian Navy. Admiral Hagen is well known for a number of unsavory reasons, not the least of which is his desire to promote Air-to-Sea military operations. Both appointments are expected to soothe nerves on both sides of Prussia's political environment.

Extraordinary Facts in Fiction
True Historical Details

PIERRE-JULES HETZEL
15 JANUARY 1814 – 17 MARCH 1886

Despite all that you have observed in these pages, dear reader, you may be shocked to learn that the real Monsieur Hetzel was merely a gentleman and publisher in the mid to late 19th Century. We can assure you that he was emphatically not a bio-mechanical person in charge of a frightening array of enhanced men. He was a friend and publisher to Jules Verne – together they made each other's careers. Monsieur Hetzel was indeed a French patriot, a well-known republican, though history credits him more with his numerous artistic successes than political courage.

We here at Gray's Gazettes salute the Pierre-Jules Hetzel of reality and thank him for allowing us to borrow his name and a few of his circumstances. We would encourage you, dear reader, to explore the history of this gentleman's true life and times.

THE FLOCKMOCKER ALL-IN-ONE PASSENGER LOCOMOTIVE
(or, as it was correctly known)
THE 1910 MCKEEN RAILMOTOR

With a hat's off salute to the McKeen Company of Omaha, Nebraska, we were thrilled to find such a marvel of engineering to inspire Professor Flockmocker. The McKeen Railmotor was a self-propelled railcar that was designed for and originally operated by the Union Pacific Railroad. The designer was one Mr. Edward H. Harriman, who introduced the first model in 1904. Two variations were put into production: a 65-passenger model and a 105-passenger model. The Railmotors were quite elegant, consisting of a single unit, with passenger seating in the rear and the gasoline powered motor in the front. The Railmotor also sported an aerodynamic profile and round porthole windows. For the time, it was a fast, flexible, and affordable means of travel, quite popular in the United States and Australia. The Railmotor was slowly replaced by even cheaper-to-run diesel locomotives and eliminated as a result of the decline in passenger train travel. However, dear reader, we prefer to suggest credit to Professor Flockmocker who was, according to him, always ahead of his time – thus he was never late.

GRAY'S ONE SHILLING STORIES, NOVELS, & GAZETTES

Presents to our Readers
Upcoming publications of exceptional Quality

From Our Sister Publication
Get the latest copy!

And the very latest in amazing adventure, shocking thrills, remarkable technology, and heart-breaking romance from these extraordinary authors

Action! Adventure! Science!

- Read the amazing story of Professor Nicodemus Boffin and how he saved the good name of his mentor, the great British scientist Michael Faraday.
- Learn how Boffin's bitter rival, the Viscount Whitehall-Barnes, sought to steal a secret notebook in which Faraday had described incomprehensible experimental results.
- Thrill at how Boffin struggles to thwart the nefarious Viscount, protect his family, and preserve the legacy of his mentor.

The very latest page-turning thriller from **Mike Tierney**
THE SECRET NOTEBOOK OF MICHAEL FARADAY!

ROMANCE!

Diana Corbett's childhood was plagued by unceasing dreams of smoke and flames. The nightmares went away, until the noted travel writer's first night on assignment in Louisiana … when they returned with a vengeance. Could the handsome Cajun, Amos Boudreaux, be the key to unlocking the secret of

BAYOU FIRE?

Award-winning author **Sharon E. Cathcart** brings you her first full-length historical paranormal tale, set against the backdrops of modern-day and 1830s New Orleans.

A Volcano Lady Novel by T.E. MacArthur

IMAGINE

An alternate steampunk history where ghosts and demons are a normal part of life. Families known as the Great Houses control the economy of the Great States of America and the middle class and the lower class Irish sole purpose is to not only to serve them, but to rid their lives of supernatural beings.

Compiled together for the first time are seven stories based on the popular steampunk comic Boston Metaphysical Society. The collection includes Steampunk Rat and The Demons of Liberty Row, in addition to the short stories, The Clockwork Man and The Way Home

All stories are prequels to the comic and contain no spoilers. The book also includes line art by Emily Hu.

THE BOSTON METAPHYSICAL SOCIETY: PRELUDE
by Madeleine Holly-Rising
Get your copy now!

THE DARK VICTORIAN

Meet Secret Commission agents, Artifice the artificial ghost and Jim Dastard, the animated skull.

Together, the two resurrected criminals with pasts unknown fight the monstrous evils that plague an 1880's mechanical and supernatural London. Artifice recalls nothing before her death, but can three women–a mad journalist, a mysterious woman in black, and a prostitute–rekindle love before Art dies again?

Mystery abounds in this latest novel
by Elizabeth Watasin
RISEN

PARIS 1880, THE CITY OF LIGHT

Clockwork nobles of the Court promenade through the halls of Versailles, while Watcher spheres and cyborg police menace citizens in the streets.

Adelaide, the Royal Physician Scientist works frantically on an automaton designed to replace the failing sovereigns, but will it be ready in time to save the monarchy? In the cafes of Montmartre, Henri paints the common people chafing under the reign of the Augmented monarchs and dreams of a France free of machines. John yearns to capture the essence of beauty in his paintings with the luminous Marie-Ange his muse—and handmaid to the ancient Queen of France. With his brother Henri entangled in revolution, he must choose between the artificial beauty of Court and the movement to restore France.

How much humanity can be lost before you are no longer human?

The answer can only be found in
THE ARCHIMEDEAN HEART
by B.J. Sikes.

LONDON WHERE IT ALL BEGAN
The Hardcover Book

You asked for it and here it is. A full-color illustrated hardcover of "London, Where It All Began," the first book in our serialized penny-dreadful is brought to life through the color illustrations of eight talented illustrators: Martina Cecilla, Tess Fowler, David Izaguirre & Andrea Orenday, Brian Kesinger, Rocky Ormsby-Olivares, Otto Pessanha, and Jeffrey Vaca.
by David L. Drake & Katherine L. Morse.
THE ADVENTURES OF
DRAKE AND McTROWELL

DON'T FORGET YOUR VERY OWN COPY OF THE

T. E. MacArthur is an author, artist, and historian living in the San Francisco Bay Area with her new companion, Calypso the cat. She received her Bachelor's Degree in History from Cal State University and spent many an evening in subsequent Anthropology, Geology, Criminal Investigation and Art classes. Writing remains, however, her passion. She has written for several local and specialized publications and was even an accidental sports reporter for Reuters International News.

The Volcano Lady: Volumes I - IV follow the adventures of Victorian lady scientist Lettie Gantry, through the worlds of Jules Verne and History. **The Gaslight Adventures** novellas continue the thrilling adventures of Tom Turner, in the time-honored cliffhangers of dime novels, penny dreadfuls, and weekly serials. To put it mildly, T.E. has a love for all things Victorian (history and clothing from 1870 – 1890 in particular) and is having a lifelong affair with the writings of Jules Verne.

For fun, facts and giveaways:

http://VolcanoLady1.wordpress.com (http://blog.volcanolady.com.)

Made in the USA
San Bernardino, CA
16 April 2017